THE THING OF A
THOUSAND SHAPES
AND OTHER TALES FROM THE PULPS

THE THING OF A THOUSAND SHAPES

AND OTHER TALES FROM THE PULPS

OTIS ADELBERT KLINE

WILDSIDE PRESS

Published by Wildside Press LLC.
wildsidepress.com | bcmystery.com

CONTENTS

INTRODUCTION

Otis Adelbert Kline (1891-1946) worked as an author and literary agent during the pulp era. Much of his fiction first appeared in pulp magazines such as *Strange Stories*, *Argosy*, *Oriental Stories,* and *Weird Tales*. Kline was an amateur orientalist and a student of Arabic, like his friend and sometime collaborator, E. Hoffmann Price, and he drew on his research for exotic backgrounds for his stoires.

However, in spite of an impressive body of work, Kline is best known these days for an imaginary literary feud with Tarzan author Edgar Rice Burroughs. Kline supposedly gained Burroughs's enmity by producing close imitations of Burroughs' work, such as *The Planet of Peril* (1929) and its two sequels—both highly reminiscent of Burroughs' Martian novels, though set on Venus. Burroughs, according to the story, promptly retaliated by writing his own Venus novels, whereupon Kline responded with an even more direct imitation of Burroughs's work—a pair of adventure novels set on Mars. Kline's jungle adventure stories, reminiscent of Burroughs' Tarzan tales, have also been cited as evidence of the conflict.

While both authors did write the works in question, the theory that they did so in contention with each other is supported only circumstantially, reflected most in their thematic resemblance and the publication dates. The feud theory was originally set forth in a fan press article, "The Kline-Burroughs War," by Donald A. Wollheim (*Science Fiction News*, November, 1936), and afterward given wider circulation by Sam Moskowitz in his book *Explorers of the Infinite* (1963). Richard A. Lupoff thoroughly debunked the feud, however, in his book *Edgar Rice Burroughs: Master of Adventure* (1965). Among the evidence cited by Lupoff: (1) no comment from either writer acknowledging the feud is documented, and (2) family members of the two authors have no recollection of ever hearing them mention it. Further, Wollheim stated, when questioned on the source of his own information: "I made it up!"

In the mid-1930s, Kline largely abandoned writing to concentrate on his career as a literary agent (most famously for fellow *Weird Tales* author Robert E. Howard, creator of Conan the Barbarian). Kline represented Howard from the spring of 1933 till Howard's death in June 1936, and he continued to act as literary agent for Howard's estate thereafter. It has been suggested that Kline may have completed Howard's novel *Almuric*, which he submitted to *Weird Tales* for posthumous publication in 1939, although this claim is disputed.

"The Dragoman's Secret" originally appeared in the Spring, 1931 issue of *Oriental Stories* magazine, a companion to *Weird Tales* also edited by Farnsworth Wright. *Oriental Stories* presented a mix of fantasy and historical adventure with Asian and Middle Eastern themes, with writers drawing on the Arabian Nights and many other sources for exotic material. Not only Kline, but many *Weird Tales* authors contributed to its pages, no doubt encouraged by editor Farnsworth Wright.

—Karl Wurf
Rockville, Maryland

THE DRAGOMAN'S SECRET

1

I have found that there are but three kinds of women in the world, *effendi*: those whose memory readily departs from us; those whose memory we deliberately put away from us; and those who, were we to live beyond the age of a thousand, we could never forget.

Such a woman was Mariam—a pearl of great price and a jewel among a million—yet for that she was not of the true faith, I nightly ask Allah to forgive me for cherishing her memory. I have had many singular and startling adventures, but none to quite compare with those which befell me when Mariam came into my life.

You would hear the tale, *effendi*? It is one which I have never dared relate to a Moslem; yet I have longed, these many years, to unbosom myself to an understanding friend. You are of a different faith, and might sympathize. But can I trust you with the secret?

Well then, here is the coffee shop at Silat, where we can sit in privacy and comfort, away from the glare of the noonday sun.

Ho, Silat! Two *shishas* stuffed to overflowing with the best Syrian leaf, and coffee, bitter as aloes, black as a Nubian at midnight, and hot as the hinges of *Johannim's* innermost gate.

Aihee! You, who know me as Hamed bin Ayyub, the bent and wrinkled dragoman, should have seen me in the days of my youth—tall and straight as a Rudaynian lance, with hair of raven blackness, a bold and handsome countenance, and the heart of a lion. Those were the days when rare and interesting adventures befell me.

As I told you, *effendi*, I have at times attained considerable wealth. There was one time when, through a series of singular circumstances, I fell heir to the wealth, the home, and the beautiful slave girl of a rich young goldsmith.

For two years I lived with her in great joy and happiness, at the end of which time she bore me a daughter. But when she presented me with the child, Allah saw fit to receive my beloved into His clemency.

As I was unable to care for the child, I fared with her to the house of my uncle, who graciously took her into his *harim*, and whose women gave her loving care. Then, as my bosom was constricted with sorrow, and my mind so distracted with grief that I no longer had the power of peace, I sold my house and all that it contained, and having converted all my wealth into gold, purchased a camel with a *shugduf* litter and left the city for the purpose of making the pilgrimage to Mecca.

The Jerusalem caravan had already departed, but the great caravan from Damascus was on its way, and I knew that by crossing El Ghor, the Jordan, and camping for a day or two on the Hajj Road until it came up, I would be able to join it.

But alas for the plans of men when they run contrary to the will of Allah Almighty. It was written that I should not complete my pilgrimage, for the first day of my journey had not yet ended when I was beset by a band of fierce *harami*, whose contemptible livelihood is gained by plundering honest men.

I drew my simitar and fought desperately, sending two of their black souls to scorch in *Johannim*. But I was tumbled from my camel by a cowardly blow from behind which laid my head open, and would have split it as a knife divides a melon had not my turban been stuffed with gold pieces.

Not content with taking my camel and my treasure, those greedy and murderous dogs actually stripped the clothing from my body, leaving me naked and apparently dying, as food for the vultures and jackals. In this condition I swooned away.

* * * *

When my senses returned to me, I first became conscious of a swaying, lurching motion, which apprised me that I was riding on the back of a camel.

I opened my eyes, and my senses whirled and were like to leave me once more at what I beheld. For bending over me, her gaze solicitous and tender, was a ravishingly beautiful young girl. Her eyes were twin stars of loveliness. The purity and whiteness of her alabaster brow put the beauty of the crescent moon to shame. Her cheeks combined the velvety softness of the peach with the delicate tint of new-blown roses. And her lips were redder than new wine, with seductive curves that were more intoxicating.

But my eyes were not destined to feast on her loveliness for more than a moment, for as soon as she saw that my senses had returned she quickly veiled her face with a blush of becoming modesty.

I closed my eyes once more, pretending to sleep, but glancing at her from time to time beneath my lowered lids. Upon finding that I could not beguile her into lowering her veil by this subterfuge, I was about to give off shamming and speak to her, when there suddenly resounded near at hand the wild shouts of raiders, mingled with the reports of firearms and the clash of blades.

The girl gave a little scream of terror as the curtain of the litter was ripped aside by a huge black hand, and a giant eunuch, longer than lumber and broader than a bench, mounted on a tall dromedary with magnificent trappings, leered in at us, rolling the whites of his eyes horribly, his blubber lips drawn back in a hideous grin.

"*Salam aleykum*, Mariam Khatun," he mouthed. "I, Suwayd, the humble slave of Khallaf al Tamim, bring you greetings from my illustrious master."

"Back to your master, black dog!" she retorted. "Tell him that I am not for such desert scum as he, nor do I fear him. Let him release my servants and permit me to resume my journey, and all will be overlooked. But if he persist in his evil intentions, then will death morn with him in the morning and night with him in the night, nor will he or those who ride with him, live long to boast of this foul misdeed."

The eunuch chuckled contemptuously.

"Not for nothing is my master named 'Khallaf al Tamim,' " he said. "Khallaf the Strong takes what pleases him without fear or favor. He but sent his humble slave to ascertain if you were really the Lady Mariam."

So saying, he suddenly tore off her face veil.

During this conversation I had been lying back on my side of the litter, unnoticed by the eunuch, but at sight of this outrage, Allah vouchsafed me strength to sit up. Jerking the veil from his grasp and catching him by the throat, I said:

"For this base act, O ugly abortion of a mangy hyena, you die!"

"Not by your hand, O whelp of a rabid wolf!" he replied, easily twisting my hand away and then jerking me across the girl's lap and completely out of the litter. Weakened as I was by the loss of blood from my wound, I was as a babe in the hands of the black giant, who bent me back over his knees and coolly drew his *jambiyah* to slit my throat.

At this moment there rode up beside us a huge, dark-skinned, black-bearded fellow, nearly as large as the eunuch who held me, and almost as black. He was richly dressed, and armed to the teeth, and bestrode a milk-white she-dromedary worth a small fortune in any *souk* in the land. I recognized him instantly from his description as Khallaf al Tamim, a *Jabarti* or Moslem Abyssinian, leader of a band of desperate cutthroats whose depredations were spoken of with awe and trembling wherever men gathered. He was reputed to have a large and magnificent *harim* in Hail, and to be under the protection of the Sharif of the Wahabis.

"What is that, Suwayd, which you have pulled from the litter of the Lady Mariam?" he asked.

"A cowardly son of flight who crept in to hide," replied the eunuch with the keen blade of his weapon against my gullet.

"A moment, Suwayd," said Khallaf. "I will tell you when to cut his throat. Let us first learn who he is."

The eunuch, who was evidently a blood-thirsty villain, mumbled something to himself, and his master reined his white dromedary between us and the litter. Lifting the curtain, he looked in, and I observed that Mariam had replaced her face-veil.

"Allah's peace and blessing upon you, Mariam Khatun," he said deferentially. "Your slave, Khallaf al Tamim, would learn if the life of this young dog of a *Badawi* is of value to you."

"No peace and no welcome to you, O black African monkey," she replied spiritedly. "Release him and those of my slaves and followers your scurvy cutthroats have left alive, that I may resume my journey."

"That I can not do, O lady," replied Khallaf, "much as it grieves me, your love-slave, to disobey your lightest wish. I have been commanded by the Sharif Nureddin Yusuf to bring you to Hail to stand trial for sorcery, heresy and proselyting among those of the one and true faith."

"You lie, O Jackal of Abyssinia!" she retorted. "This raid is of your own choosing and for your own purpose."

The brow of Khallaf contracted.

"Your sorcery has told you this, my lady," he said. "I will admit, then, that this expedition is of my choosing. And the reason is that, disguised as a eunuch, I saw you in the *hammam* in Jerusalem, whither I had gone in feigned attendance on one of my female slaves to learn why my women who visited the baths were so impressed by your beauty. It was there I became your love-slave, and there I resolved to possess you. And though Khallaf the Strong takes that which he desires, yet would he prefer that you come to him willingly."

"Neither willingly nor unwillingly shall Khallaf al Tamim possess me," she replied.

"For the present," he replied, "we will let it rest at that. Women are prone to change their minds with the shifting of the winds. But you have not answered my question. Is it your wish that this hider behind your skirts be kept alive?"

"He is nothing to me," she answered, "yet I would be merciful, even to a dog."

"The quality of mercy," replied Khallaf, "is an attribute of Almighty Allah. Humbler creatures, I among them, seldom possess it. Ho, Suwayd! You will take this pig away and slit his throat."

Weakened though I was, I began struggling violently in the grasp of the huge Nubian, feeling that the hour for my death had indeed come. It was true that I was nothing to this girl but a penniless, helpless wayfarer whom she had befriended, so why should she, who did not wish to be placed in the position of asking a favor from Khallaf, sue for my life?

But my struggles were as futile as though I had been a bird in the jaws of a serpent. With a grin of fiendish joy, Suwayd turned his beast to haul me a little way off, that I might not be slain within sight of the girl.

But we had scarcely started ere there came a cry from the litter of the Lady Mariam.

"Stop! Do not slay him."

"Oh, ho!" said Khallaf, with a knowing grin. "And what is this dog to you?"

"He is—he is my brother," she faltered. "Two days ago he was wounded by raiding bandits, and I have been caring for him in my litter, on the march."

"Your brother!" he sneered. "A likely story! You who are a seventh daughter of a seventh daughter!" He shouted to a dirty, unkempt robber with a hennaed beard who stood a little way off. "Ho there, Humayd! Bring me one of the prisoners."

A moment later, the redbeard rode up, leading a *Badawin* cameleer by a rope, looped around his neck.

"Mark well what I ask you, slave," roared Khallaf, glaring down at the prisoner, "and speak only truth if you would not die where you stand."

"I hear and I obey," replied the cameleer, shaking with fright.

"Then tell me the name of this prisoner?" thundered the *Jabarti*, pointing a black finger at me.

"Alas, my lord, I know it not!" quavered the cameleer. "Two days ago we found him, sorely wounded, and robbed of all his possessions, lying naked and unconscious on the trail near the Hajj Road. My mistress took pity on him, and ordered that we clothe him from our stores and place him in her litter, that she might care for him."

"So! We begin to get the truth!" grinned Khallaf. "Take him away, Humayd."

He swung on me. "Your name, dog!" he demanded.

"You name me a dog," I replied defiantly, "so let that name suffice you, though I am not of your mongrel breed."

"What! You yap at me, cur? Well then, you shall have the treatment of any dog who snarls at his captor. Bind his hands, Suwayd.

Then let him walk beside your beast with a rope around his neck. And if he falls—"

The big Nubian grinned knowingly. Then he made his dromedary kneel, none too gently bound my hands, and put a noose around my neck. Though I was so weak I staggered like a man drugged with drink, I was dragged away with the caravan, knowing that to fall would be to die.

2

Staggering, stumbling, choking in the dust from a hundred camels' hooves, I managed to keep my feet as I walked beside the mount of the huge eunuch with a rope around my neck. My wounded head throbbed unmercifully, and I was constantly assailed by a terrific thirst, incited by my wound and augmented by the rays of the sun which beat down from the steel-blue sky with terrific heat. And to add to my afflictions, fierce biting flies and pestiferous gnats made merry with my unprotected face and hands.

The caravan stopped at noon, and I, who had been traveling on will-power alone, fell into a merciful unconsciousness. Had I been forced to continue but a few moments longer, my life had been forfeit by the rope.

When my senses came to me once more it was evening. I was lying, unbound, among the other prisoners. They offered me coffee and freshly baked bread, which I took gratefully. After I had eaten, the cameleer who had been questioned by Khallaf, lent me his *chibuk* and a pinch of tobacco. After smoking, I returned the pipe to its owner, and pillowing my head on my arm, fell asleep beside the fading embers of the fire.

It seemed that I had not slept more than a moment, when I was aroused, bound, haltered, and led away once more by Suwayd, the eunuch.

My strength had been increased by food and rest, and the night was cool, for which I thanked Almighty Allah as I trudged along with the caravan.

We traveled until dawn, prayed the dawn prayer, made coffee and bread, and after a brief rest, pressed onward until noon.

For many days and nights we continued thus, traveling from midnight until noon, and resting from noon until midnight. At the end of that time, we came to Hail, the Wahabi stronghold in the midst of the Nefud desert.

During all this time I had not been permitted to see or speak to my beautiful young benefactress. But she was constantly in my thoughts, nor did I wonder that Khallaf, or any other man who had seen her charms, had become her love-slave, for I was more sorely smitten than ever before or since. If, when I have been received into the mercy of Allah, I find a *Huriyah* of the Virgins of Paradise, who is but half as beautiful as she, then will I be content, and praise Allah forever.

We were hurried to the house of Khallaf, and I down to a damp and evil-smelling cell in the night-black dungeon beneath it.

I was well aware of the fact that the Abyssinian ruffian would not have kept me alive for a moment, had he not thought to fit me into his plans. He believed that my life was of value to Mariam— that by threatening her with my death he might win her consent if not her desire, to enter his *harim*.

And so I laid a plan of my own. I did not know to what length the girl might go to save my miserable life. I did know that she had condescended to request it of this black monster whom she despised, and that I was thus twice beholden to her for my very existence. Being a man of honor, there were but two things for me to do in the circumstances. I must either escape from Khallaf, or take my own life. My plans were made accordingly.

The only entrance to the dungeon was guarded by an aged, hook-nosed, gray-bearded Wahabi, who spent much of his time sitting on the bottom step of the stairway, smoking his *chibuk*. At irregular intervals he patrolled the corridor, casting the yellow rays of his lantern into each of the cells and examining the inmates.

I waited until I judged it must be near midnight, then went to the bars of my cell and waited for him to make his next inspection. He came, presently, shuffling along in his loose slippers and puffing at his *chibuk*. He started back a little when he saw me staring at him through the bars, but I called to him reassuringly.

"Come close, uncle. I have a message for your ears alone."

"What dark secrets you have, keep to yourself, O pig who prays without washing," he replied.

"Nay, but good uncle," I persisted, "this is to your advantage, but it would not be were I to shout it through the corridors."

At this, he came a trifle closer.

"I have here," I said, indicating my handkerchief, a corner of which I had knotted and thrust into my sash, "a precious jewel worth a king's ransom—a jewel that will buy you your heart's desire, be it whatsoever it may."

"You lie," he mouthed, but an avaricious gleam had crept into his eyes, and I knew that he half believed me. "But had you such a jewel, what would that profit me?"

"Come closer and I will tell you," I replied.

He stepped up more closely and I drew the handkerchief from my sash.

"The jewel for my freedom," I whispered to him.

"First let me see it," he replied, holding the lantern high.

"Here, look for yourself," I said, and thrust both hands through the bars of my cell door, extending the handkerchief toward him and making as if I were endeavoring to undo the knot.

He bent over eagerly, holding the lantern still higher. In a trice I had the handkerchief twisted around his neck, the ends drawn taut, so that he could not cry out, but only made queer, gurgling noises.

"The door!" I said, fiercely. "Unlock it quickly, and do not reach for your simitar or cry out—or you die!"

He fumbled for the key, while I gave him just enough air to keep him conscious, and presently finding it, inserted it in the lock and turned it. As the door swung inward, I dragged the half-choked guard in with it.

To bind and gag him, and take his simitar, was but the work of a moment. I then locked him in the cell, picked up his lantern and quickly made my way up the stairs.

On reaching the top of the stairs, I cautiously opened the door a little way. Just in front of me was a hallway, at one side of which a fat *bowab* snored on a low *diwan*. Beyond him was the door which I knew led into the garden.

Leaving my lantern behind and drawing my simitar, I edged past the door. Closing it softly behind me and watching the *bowab* with bated breath, I tiptoed to the next door. It was closed by a huge bar, which I succeeded in sliding back without noise. Then I opened it, stepped out into the night, and closed it noiselessly.

* * * *

The garden was bathed in moonlight, and the sweet scent of blossoms was like a breath of Paradise after the stench of the dungeon from which I had just escaped. I was thirsty, and in the center of the garden a fountain splashed musically. But I forgot its allure when I saw a tall figure, carrying a long rifle, arise from beside it and slowly walk toward the garden gate.

Crouching low, I crept through the shrubbery until I was beside the path along which the guard was sauntering. His crunching footfalls drew nearer—passed me. The path was bordered with whitewashed stones. One of these I caught up, and leaping out behind him, brought it down on his head. His knees crumpled under him, and he fell in a heap. I caught his rifle to prevent the noise of its falling, and laid it beside him.

Divesting him of his head-cloth and burnoose, I donned them, and taking up his rifle, walked to the gate. I stood there for a moment, leaning on the rifle and looking about as a guard might have done, but seeing no one in the garden, I quickly slid back the bar and stepped out into the street.

Once out of the garden, I walked swiftly, not knowing in what direction I was going, but bent on putting as much distance as possible between me and the house of Khallaf before my escape should be discovered.

Scarcely had I passed the limit of the garden wall, ere I met a stranger, who saluted me with the "*Salam*," and asked if I could direct him to the house of Khallaf. Afraid to arouse his suspicions by hurrying on, I paused to answer his question.

But at this moment I heard a stealthy footfall behind me, and knew that I was in a trap. I tired to whirl and engage my unseen antagonist, but a heavy, evil-smelling sack was drawn over my head and arms, and I was thrown to the ground. Then my hands and feet were securely bound, and I was carried for a short distance up a few steps and through a door into a building where the footfalls of my abductors echoed hollowly, as if it were unfurnished.

One of my captors greeted some one with the words: "*Ishtar Baraket,*" which means: "Ishtar bless thee," and was answered in kind. Then I knew that I was not in the hands of godly men, but had fallen into the clutches of idolaters and casters of magic spells.

Presently I heard a gruff voice say:

"You have him? That is well. He is said to be a close-mouthed fool, but the cords and a few hot coals will set his tongue to clacking."

3

With the foul-smelling sack still over my head, I was carried through several rooms, and finally put down on a hard tile floor. Then the sack was taken off, and I faced a group of stern-visaged men, dressed like the Wahabis, but evidently not of them, for of all the Arabs, the Wahabis are the most strict believers.

One of them, a huge, thick-waisted fellow with Persian features and a wiry, iron-gray beard, said:

"What have you done with the Lady Mariam? Where is she concealed? Speak quickly and truthfully, O slave of the Black Jackal, or it will be the worse for you."

"I have done nothing with her," I replied.

The big Persian pointed significantly toward two stout cords which depended from a rafter above my head, and to a pan of glowing charcoal near by.

"Will you speak without these?" he asked.

"She was captured by Khallaf al Tamim," I replied, "but I know not where she is concealed."

"We know she was captured by your Jinn-mad master," he replied, "and you know where she was hidden. For the last time I bid you speak."

"Khallaf is not my master," I answered. "I was traveling with the caravan of the Lady Mariam when he captured it. Just now, I escaped from his clutches, only to be made prisoner by your men."

"That is a lie," he snarled. "Too often have I seen the Black Jackal's garden *bowab* not to recognize you. We will see if the cords and coals will bring the truth to your tongue."

Despite my protests and struggles, my shoes were removed and I was strung up by the thumbs, so that the tips of my toes barely touched the floor. I gripped the cords with my hands, thus drawing myself a few inches higher, and easing my thumbs, but one can not hold himself up thus for a long time. Just as I was beginning to tire, and would have let myself down on my toes, the Persian pushed the pan of glowing charcoal beneath them.

A moment more, and the cords were cutting deeply into my fingers, while the heat from the charcoal scorched my feet painfully. I drew them up, and the motion sunk the cords deeper into my fingers.

"Now will you speak?" asked the Persian.

"I can not tell you what you ask," I groaned.

"You will beg to be allowed to tell me soon, O father of lies," he replied.

Presently my fingers relaxed. Human flesh could stand no more. A searing pain told me my toes had touched the charcoal. I drew them up, but the motion increased the strain on my aching thumbs.

Just then a man entered the room. He saluted all present with the greeting of the idolaters: "*Ishtar Baraket.*" And they replied in kind. Then he seated himself beside the huge Persian, and glanced up at me. Our recognition was simultaneous, for he was the cameleer who had befriended me in the caravan, and who had evidently escaped from Khallaf as he entered the town.

"Why do you torture this man?" he asked the Persian.

"He is the gate-keeper of Khallaf," replied that worthy, "and we would learn from him the secret of where our lady is confined."

"Then cut him down," said the cameleer, "for he can not tell you. He is the wounded pilgrim whom our mistress befriended."

"You are positive?"

"By my head and beard!"

The Persian kicked the pan of charcoal from under me, and with his keen *jambiyah* severed the cords. So overcome was I with pain and exhaustion that I slumped to the floor. One of the ruffians tossed my shoes to me, and I donned them with great difficulty and pain because of my blistered feet and lacerated hands. Then, at a sign from the Persian, one of the men helped me to my feet and led me into another room.

For some time he remained there with me, and I heard the murmur of voices, so low that I could only catch a word now and then. But I gathered that they were trying to decide what to do with me. That I now knew them for members of that secret cult which all true Moslems despise, made me extremely dangerous to them. Yet there were some who feared to do away with me because I had been befriended by their mistress, and they might thus bring down her wrath on their heads.

Presently the talking grew louder—became a Babel. The evil crew seemed about evenly divided as to whether I should be kept alive, or slain.

At length, those who would have me slain won, and I heard the gruff voice of the Persian, as he ordered me strangled and buried in the garden.

When I heard this sentence, I sprang up, and dodging the man who had been sent with me, bounded through the rear door. I came out into the garden, but was pounced upon by a guard stationed there. A moment more and the man I had eluded came running out accompanied by another who had been chosen to act as my executioner.

This man, who had been ordered to strangle me, carried a thin, stout cord in his hands. While the others held me, he made the strangler's loop and came up to cast it over my head.

Life was dear to me, and I was desperate. So as my executioner approached I kicked him in the belly and at the same time flung out my arms, throwing over the two men who held me. The wall was but a few feet away, and I reached it in an instant. Leaping up, I caught its rim with my lacerated fingers, drew myself up, and dropped to freedom on the other side.

Like a frightened hare, I scuttled off down the street, not knowing which way to run, but bent only on getting as far from that den of ruffians as possible. I had scarcely taken twenty steps, however, when I heard a great hullabaloo behind me, and loud cries of: "Stop thief! Catch the robber!"

By this time, morning had just dawned, and the call to prayer was sounding from the minaret of a near-by mosque. A few people were stirring in the street, and all of these, aroused by the cries of my pursuers, sought to detain me and joined in the chase. Soon I had a crowd of more than fifty people after me, all shouting: "Stop thief!" at the top of their voices. Stones and tiles were hurled at me from roof-tops, and snarling curs snapped at my heels. Presently a youth stuck his foot out from a doorway and tripped me. As I fell, a score of persons pounced on me.

I was dragged to my feet by the big Persian who had ordered my death a short time before, and who seemed bent on accomplishing it in public now. Two of his henchmen held my arms, while he led the cries of: "Death to the thief! Stone him!" which came from the throats of the multitude. A stone whizzed past my ear, and some one threw an overripe pomegranate with poor aim, for it missed me and struck the Persian full in the mouth.

A second stone bruised my shoulder, and a third struck my chest, knocking the breath from my body. I am positive that all would have ended for me, then and there, had not the *wali* and his watch come up at that moment.

* * * *

The *wali*, a tall, important-looking individual with a large turban and a bushy gray beard, strode into the center of the disturbance with his stout fellows knocking the rabble right and left.

"What is this brawl?" he demanded.

"We have captured a thief," said the Persian.

"By whose testimony?"

"Mine and others."

"Well then, take him before the *kazi*, that he may be judged according to the law. If he is found guilty he will pay the penalty soon enough without the aid of your sticks and stones."

He signed to two of his burly fellows, who seized my arms and dragged me away.

The *kazi*, a short, pot-bellied Wahabi, whose round and rubicund countenance showed the effect of much good living with little endeavor, stared at me for a moment and said:

"Of what is this man accused? And who will bear witness against him?"

"I bear witness," said the Persian. "He is a thief."

I had it on the point of my tongue to denounce the Persian and his companions as idolaters, and thus not only win the sympathy of the crowd, but compass the destruction of my enemies. Then I suddenly remembered that these fellows, no matter what they had done to me, were the followers of Mariam engaged in an attempt to rescue her from the clutches of Khallaf. It followed that to denounce them would be to lessen if not absolutely to cut off her hope of rescue. I resolved, therefore, that no matter what happened, the identity of these men would not be revealed by me.

"You say this man is a thief," said the *kazi*, addressing the Persian. "What has he stolen?"

"Why, just now he stole my head-cloth and burnoose from my house, and escaped over my garden wall."

"You lie, swine of Iran!" I retorted. "A Persian pig never wore clothing such as this."

"I have worn them for a year, O stench!" he said.

"You saw them for the first time today, O offal!" I answered.

"May your falsehoods return and throttle you, O liar!"

"May your beard turn to a nest of maggots and devour your lying tongue!"

"Enough of this abuse!" said the *kazi*, sternly. "You, Persian, say that this *Badawi* stole your headcloth and burnoose. Have you recovered them?"

"No, O fount of wisdom. He still wears them."

"But how am I to know that he wears your headcloth and cloak?"

"I testify that they are the property of Maksoud, the Persian," cried one of the men who had captured me.

"And I," cried the other, "also certify that they are Maksoud's property."

"The Sunni law," said the *kazi*, thoughtfully stroking his beard, "ordains that for an offense of this kind, a man must part with his right hand. Take the prisoner, therefore, and strike off his right hand, seeing that the wound be properly seared so he will not bleed to death."

"We hear and obey, O paragon of understanding," replied the two burly ruffians who held me, and were about to hurry me away to carry out the sentence when there was a clatter of hoofs and a company of horsemen rode up. At their head was Khallaf the *Jabarti*.

"Way for Khallaf the Strong!" cried the people. "Way for the blood-brother of our lord, the Sharif!"

"What is this, *kazi*?" asked Khallaf, reining his Awasil mare to a sliding halt. "Where got you this man?"

"Just now he was brought to me, accused of thievery, excellency," replied the *kazi*, "and I have sentenced him to pay the penalty according to the Sunni law."

"The fellow is an escaped slave of mine," said Khallaf. "Turn him over to me, and I will be responsible for him, and for his ample punishment."

"I hear and I obey, O protector of the poor and blood-brother of our Sharif," replied the *kazi*, respectfully.

Two of Khallaf's men quickly dismounted, and after binding my hands behind me, threw me over a saddle-bow.

The Abyssinian was about to ride away when he suddenly spied in the crowd the cameleer who had befriended me on the march, and who had later identified me to the followers of Mariam.

"Seize me that man!" roared Khallaf, and it was no sooner said than done. The cameleer was bound and thrown over a saddle-bow, and the cavalcade moved away.

4

Back at the house of Khallaf, I was thrown into the selfsame cell from which I had escaped the night before. But this time, the *Jabarti* took no chances. In addition to the old hook-nosed Wahabi who patrolled the corridor, a burly guard stood, naked simitar in hand, in front of my cell door.

I asked for food and drink, and was given a crust of stale bread and a cup of water.

Several hours later I was led from my cell, each arm held by a powerful warrior, and taken into a magnificently furnished room—the *salamlik* or reception room of the Abyssinian. He was seated on a luxuriously cushioned *diwan*, smoking a *shisha*, while one lissom slave girl fanned him with a palm leaf and another proffered sherbet and coffee on a golden tray.

"Bind the dog to the pillar at my right," directed Khallaf.

I was hurried forward, and my hands were drawn back as far as they would reach around the thick pillar, and made fast with a cord.

A moment later the cameleer was brought in. At the order of the *Jabarti* he was similarly bound to the pillar at the left of the *diwan*.

Khallaf took a sip of sherbet from a tiny golden cup.

"Away, all of you," he said, "and send Suwayd to me."

The four warriors and two slave girls departed, and shortly thereafter the huge black eunuch entered, carrying a brazier in which charcoal smoldered, and a small pair of bellows. A long simitar hung at his side, and two curved *jambiyahs* were stuck in his sash. On his ebony features was a look of such pleased anticipation that I knew he was about to commit some act of fiendish cruelty.

"Heat the pincers, my faithful servant," directed the *Jabarti*, "and while they are heating, slit the throat of this cameleer. He must be gotten out of the way quickly, as we have other important business at hand."

"Harkening and obedience, excellency," said the huge Nubian with a broad grin.

He put the brazier on the floor and began blowing the charcoal with the bellows. Projecting from the coals were the long handles of a pair of pincers.

When he had the coals glowing brightly, the eunuch put down his bellows, and rising, walked toward the cowering cameleer. Deliberately he drew a *jambiyah* from his sash, and tested the keenness of its edge with his thumb, while the poor fellow alternately wept and pleaded for his life.

Suddenly he stepped up to the doomed man, and seizing his beard with his left hand, tilted his head back, exposing his throat. The unfortunate wretch uttered a gurgling shriek as the keen blade was drawn across his gullet.

The big Nubian stood there for a moment unconcernedly; then he released his grip on the beard, permitting the lifeless head to fall forward.

"A good stroke, Suwayd," said Khallaf. "Now make ready to deal with the other."

The eunuch once more bent beside his brazier, and blew the charcoal up to a blaze with the bellows.

Then the Abyssinian clapped his hands, and a shapely young girl, swathed in diaphanous *harim* garments, was led in by a black female.

"Welcome, Mariam Khatun," said Khallaf. "I have at last captured the young *Badawi* in whose welfare you are so deeply interested. You will be seated here at my feet, that you may witness what occurs to those who oppose my will."

"I sit at your feet? I?" retorted the girl. "To sit at the feet of a baboon would be preferable. I will stand."

So saying, she wrenched her wrist from the grasp of the black female, who was attempting to drag her before the *diwan,* and dealt her a buffet across her ear that sent her sprawling.

"Let be, Lenah," said Khallaf laughingly to the black girl, "and depart."

Scrambling to her feet, the negress salaamed to her master, and hastily left the room.

"And you, little tigress," said Khallaf, "may stand if you wish, as you can see what happens to this presumptuous *Badawi* standing as well as sitting. First, his tongue, which has named me a mongrel dog, will be torn out by the roots with hot pincers. Then his eyes, which have dared to aspire to the woman of Khallaf the Strong, will be gouged out with the red-hot blade of a *jambiyah*. After which, when a sufficient time has elapsed for him to appreciate the full enormity of his misdeeds, his throat will be cut, even as that of yonder cowardly cameleer."

"Is there no help for it, but that you perpetrate this foul injustice?" she asked. "That you torture and murder an innocent man?"

"Why, as to that, it lies within your province to say," replied the crafty Khallaf.

"*My* province?"

"None other. Remember that Khallaf the Strong is your love-slave. Requite his love, and your lightest wish will be his law."

The eyes of Mariam flashed fire above her white *yashmak*.

"As to that, O great black gorilla," she said, "I should prefer to share his torture and death."

"Perhaps you will change your mind after you have witnessed his agonies," said Khallaf. "Proceed, Suwayd."

The big Nubian, who had been industriously plying his bellows during this conversation, now pulled the pincers from the brazier. Their jaws glowed white-hot as he advanced toward me with a look of fiendish delight.

Seizing the point of my jaw with his left hand, he pushed it down. I moved my head with it, keeping my mouth tightly closed, whereupon he held the hot pincers beneath the end of my nose, causing me to jerk my head back. My mouth flew open, and he inserted the pincers between my teeth, holding them apart, and searing my lips and tongue.

"Now, my loud-talking youth," he said, "we'll have your tongue in a moment."

He was peering into my mouth and spreading the jaws of the pincers when, like the very tigress Khallaf had named her, Mariam bounded to my rescue. In her hand was a slender dagger she had snatched from her bosom. It rose and fell, buried to the hilt in the breast of Suwayd, who with a loud shriek and a look of horror on his face, slumped to the floor, the pincers clattering from his hand.

Whipping out his simitar, the Abyssinian leaped to his feet just as Mariam cut the rope that held my arms around the pillar.

The hilt of Suwayd's simitar projected from beneath his huge carcass. I seized it, and came on guard as Khallaf descended on me, a thundercloud of wrath and a demon of destruction.

Sparks flew from our clashing blades as we cut and parried, and although my antagonist was larger and stronger than I, these odds were somewhat evened by my superior skill and greater agility.

There came the sound of running and shouting from beyond the door, but in a flash Mariam had reached it and drawn the bar.

Fierce anger flared in Khallaf's eyes when he found himself unable to instantly reach me with his blade. Accustomed to cutting down men of less skill by his hammer-and-tongs methods, backed by his enormous strength, he was both astounded and annoyed by my ability to elude his terrific rain of blows, and to return them in such good measure that he was constrained to spend as much time in parrying as in cutting.

For my part, I knew that we were evenly matched for the moment, but because of my wounds and privations, his greater strength and freshness must prevail in the end.

I was reaching the limit of my endurance, when Fortune suddenly interposed in my favor, for Khallaf stepped squarely into the brazier of smoldering charcoal in which Suwayd had heated the pincers. It must have burned instantly through his paper-thin *harim* slippers, as he uttered a howl of pain, and for an instant, lowered his guard.

In that instant, I smote his neck with all my remaining strength. Allah guided and aided my arm, for his scowling black head flew off and rolled away, while his immense body pitched to the floor.

But scarcely had I rid myself of this enemy, ere the door was broken down, and a company of armed men poured in. At their head was Maksoud, the Persian, who leveled a pistol at my head and pulled the trigger.

5

Simultaneously with the report of Maksoud's pistol, there was the click of steel beneath its barrel. Mariam, seeing his purpose, had struck it upward with her bloody dagger.

"Fool!" she said. "Another move to harm this youth who is under my protection, and I'll have you laid by the heels and beaten to death with the *kurbaj*."

"I crave forgiveness, O Voice of the Great Goddess," said Maksoud, contritely. "This *Badawi* is the possessor of dangerous knowledge, and being a Moslem, might divulge it."

"As to that, I will assume all responsibility," replied the girl. "What of this black baboon's household?"

"The men are dead, my lady," said Maksoud. "The women and children are imprisoned in the *harim*."

"Lock them in the dungeons with food and water for two days," she ordered, "all except the black slave girl, Lenah. Then strip the house, and make ready for the journey."

"Harkening and obedience, O Oracle of Ishtar," replied Maksoud, and departed with his men to carry out her commands.

In an unbelievably short space of time these sons of idolatry had stripped the house of its valuables, the rich loot of Khallaf's many raids, and had made a caravan ready for departure.

Maksoud, with his face blackened and all but hidden by his *kufiyah* or head handkerchief, which he had drawn across his countenance in the manner of the *lisam*, wore a suit of Khallaf's magnificent apparel and rode his milk-white she-dromedary, thus readily passing for the Abyssinian, for they were of about the same build.

A big negro named Mustafa, who was among the followers of Mariam, wore the clothing and took the part of Suwayd the eunuch, who always accompanied his master on his journeys.

Mariam rode in a litter. Lenah the black slave girl rode in another, bound and gagged. Those of Mariam's followers who had been inhabitants of Hail, but who were now leaving it forever, made up the balance of the caravan.

Wearing *Badawin* garb, I rode the Awasil mare of Khallaf beside the lady's litter.

We had completed a day's journey, rested, and were preparing to resume the second, when Mariam called for Musayn, the *'alim*.

The graybeard came with pen, ink-case and paper, and she bade him write a note as follows:

"To Sharif Nureddin Yusuf:
Greeting!
And after, know that this, the slave girl of Khallaf the Black Jackal has been sent to you on an errand of mercy and warning. Mercy, that you release the *harim* of the *Jabarti*, whom I do not hold responsible for his crimes, and who are locked in his dungeons. Warning, that you gaze on the earthly remains of the villainous Abyssinian and his ruffians, and meditate on the fate of those who attempt to take by force a Virgin of the All-Powerful Mother Goddess.
Attempt to follow and you will be as Khallaf. Be warned, and I prophesy that you will attain The Peace,

Mariam KhatuN."

Just as our caravan departed, the slave girl was dispatched in the opposite direction with the note, riding a dromedary and carrying a day's provisions.

We traveled a five-day journey across the desert after that, until we came to a wady where I was compelled to dismount and ride in a litter blindfolded with Mustafa watching me.

At the end of the seventh day, my blindfold was removed as we entered a pleasant village situated in a grove of palm trees which was watered by a stream that trickled through a narrow valley. The houses were small, but in the center of the village there rose a great temple of the finest white marble, with pillared porticos and a dome of polished brass.

During the entire journey I had caught but fleeting glimpses of the Lady Mariam, always veiled and muffled in her traveling-clothes. But now she drew the curtain of her litter and summoned Maksoud.

"You will house this young *Badawi* in my dwelling," she directed, "while I repair to the temple to give thanks to our Great Mother Goddess for my deliverance. On your life, see that he is treated with honor and respect."

So saying, she closed the curtain of her litter and rode on, while Maksoud, who seemed little pleased with his commission, led me to a small but neat house near the temple. Here the Persian and I were ushered into the *salamlik* by an old and wrinkled eunuch who was a hunchbacked dwarf. When my conductor had made known to him the wishes of his mistress, he clapped his hands, summoning slaves, male and female, who brought us fruits, sherbets, coffee and pipes.

Presently there came to the house a messenger who spoke to the eunuch in a language I did not understand. Upon hearing his words, Maksoud excused himself and left.

I judged that the conversation had alluded to me, as both messenger and eunuch had glanced at me from time to time.

As soon as the messenger left, the eunuch clapped his hands once more, and two Mamelukes entered. To these, he gave instructions in the same strange tongue, and they hurried away.

Presently one of the Mamelukes returned, and bowing low to me, said:

"The bath is prepared, *saidi*."

"You will be pleased to accompany this slave, my lord," said the eunuch, "that you may be prepared for the test."

"The test?" I asked, bewildered. "What test?"

"All will be revealed to you in good time," said the hunchback, mysteriously.

Puzzled, I arose, and followed the Mameluke through a corridor into a room of marble and carnelian, where a hot bath had been prepared. The steam that arose from the water carried the scent of the rarest and most luxurious of perfumes.

The Mamelukes proved to be skilled bath attendants and masseurs, who scrubbed me with hot water and cold until my skin glowed with the roseate tint of a summer sunset, after which they anointed me with sweet-smelling unguents and cosmetics. Then, while the one tendered me sherbets and broths, the other dressed me in handsome and costly garments that would have done honor to an emir.

I then returned to the *salamlik*, where seven graybeards, attired in long black robes, and wearing black turbans, the fronts of which were adorned with crescent moons—symbols of Ishtar cut from mother-of-pearl—awaited me.

Then, conducted by the hunchbacked dwarf, who had in the meantime decked out his twisted body in festal array, and followed by the seven graybeards in solemn procession, I went out into the street.

From the temple, the tones of an immense gong resounded through the village in measured, throbbing cadence. Then there poured forth from the houses, and from the shops in the *souk*, men, women and children, all of whom marched to the temple, in step with the strokes of the gong.

The hunchbacked eunuch fell in step, I with him, and the graybeards who followed us did likewise.

* * * *

When we arrived at the temple we avoided the main entrance, into which the village populace was pouring, and went in by a side door. Here a hoodwink was securely fastened over my eyes. Having been warned not to touch it no matter what might occur, nor to speak unless spoken to, I was led away by two unseen conductors who held my arms on the right and left.

They took me down a stairway into what smelled like a musty subterranean animal den. Here my conductors brought me to a halt, and I distinctly heard the approaching pads of a large beast coming stealthily toward me. It stopped just in front of me and sniffed. Its fetid breath fanned my face. Then it began to make low, moaning noises, and I heard the rattle of steel.

Suddenly the hoodwink was jerked from my eyes. Standing just in front of me was a huge, black-maned African lion, rattling the bars of its cage as it endeavored to reach me with its huge paws.

My two conductors were of the black-robed fraternity, but wore, in addition, black masks that concealed all features but their eyes.

One of them spoke in solemn, sepulchral tones:

"Before you, O youth, is a dangerous path. It may lead you to love or to death. Only the great Mother Goddess knows. You are desired by the Oracle of Ishtar for the one night of love which is vouchsafed all her handmaidens by our goddess. But the final choice rests with Ishtar alone. If she accepts you, then will you consummate this love, but if she rejects you, you will die beneath the claws of this fierce beast, and its belly will be your tomb.

"You may turn back now, and escape, unhindered and unharmed, for it is written that those who come to the ordeal must do so willingly. Or you may go on, and stake your life on the issue. Consider the matter, therefore, and name your choice."

I looked at the great beast, sheathing and unsheathing its sickle claws through the bars and licking its slavering jowls in anticipation of the pleasure of rending my flesh and drinking my blood. Then I thought of the lovely Mariam, and knew that, rather than lose this lovely creature, witch and idolatress though she was, I stood ready to die not one, but a thousand deaths.

"I am ready for the ordeal," I said.

The hoodwink was drawn over my eyes once more and I was taken up the stairway into a room filled with a thousand faint rustlings and whisperings, as if it contained an immense audience who waited tensely in awe-stricken silence for something to happen. The air was heavy with the odors of sweet incense, in which I, who had been an attar, detected the sandalwood of Hind and the musk of Cathay.

Here I was helped to mount three large steps, and caused to kneel, after which my hoodwink was removed.

I was in the huge auditorium of the temple, kneeling on a wide semicircular dais that faced an immense statue of Ishtar, wrought from white marble. Save for the feeble light cast by seven candles that flickered in front of the statue, the entire room was in darkness. Just in front of the candles, seven pots of incense smoldered. Behind me, and on each side, I could hear the faint rustling and whispering which is characteristic of a large crowd tensely awaiting some unusual event.

Suddenly there sounded the low wailing of a hautboy in minor melody. It increased in volume, and was accompanied by the jingling of sistrums and the booming of kettledrums. Between the dais on which I knelt and the altar that stood before the image of the goddess, another larger dais was rising from the floor. Like the one I occupied, it was shaped like a half-moon. On this dais were seven girls, robed in flowing, translucent white garments. The one in the center stood with bowed head, arms crossed on breasts, while the three on each side of her jingled sistrums and danced a slow dance of many postures.

In front of each girl, a candle burned and a small pot of incense smoldered. As the platform came up above the level of my own, it stopped, and my heart gave a sudden bound as I recognized Mariam as the central figure of the group.

When the platform stopped, the music ceased and the girls posed as rigidly as if they had been statues. Then I heard a rustling sound behind me, and six men came up out of the darkness, three taking places on the dais on each side of me. I noticed by the candle-light from the other platform that all were dressed exactly as was I.

As soon as they took their places, Mariam turned and faced the image of the goddess. Bowing low, while the three girls on each side knelt, facing her, she said:

"Great Mother Ishtar, I have caused to be brought to thy temple the man of my heart, whom I have chosen for the night of love which thou vouchsafest all thy handmaidens. He hath signified his willingness to forfeit his life if he displeases thee, and now awaits thy pleasure and thy decision. I beseech thee, O Mother Goddess, that thou wilt grant him his life, which out of his love for me he hath placed in the balance, and thus permit thy handmaiden and thy oracle her heart's desire."

Having finished her petition, Mariam prostrated herself before the idol, and the six dancing girls did likewise.

Then there sounded from behind the immense statue, the whir of many wings, and a flock of white doves flew out above the two platforms. Once, twice, thrice, they circled. Then they slowly descended, hovering above my head and those of the six men who were on the dais with me. Presently one alighted on my shoulder. It was followed by another and another, until the entire flock of white doves had either perched on my body or alighted near me, to strut about, puffing and cooing.

Mariam did not look toward me, but somehow seemed to know just what had occurred, for she arose, and spoke once more to the image:

"Great Mother Ishtar, I thank thee."

Lights suddenly flashed on in the temple, and a great cry went up from the multitude:

"Ishtar has spoken! All glory to Ishtar!"

Mariam and I were placed side by side on a huge litter, and borne at the head of a procession to her house. Here a great feast was spread, and for several hours we acted as host and hostess. Then the guests took their leave, and we were alone.

* * * *

Of that night of love, *effendi*, my voice will ever remain silent, though my heart will always sing. It passed so swiftly that it seemed to last for but a moment, yet in it was consummated the sum of a lifetime of desire. My last memory was that, when morning dawned, I fell asleep, my head pillowed on the snowy breast of my beloved.

When I wakened, I was riding in a *shugduf* litter on the back of a camel. My head ached as if I had partaken too freely of *bhang*. Looking out, I beheld, riding ahead of me, Maksoud the Persian.

I shouted and he turned. Then he rode back and handed me the lead-rope of my camel.

"Just ahead of you," he said, "is El Ghor, and beyond that, the Jericho road to Jerusalem. The pack camel that follows you carries all the valuables of which you were robbed, for it was Khallaf the Strong who robbed you. It carries, in addition, precious stones and gold equivalent in value to half the loot taken from the Abyssinian, for it was you who slew him. Say nothing to your Moslem brethren of what has occurred to you, and so will you attain health, wealth, and the peace. *Ishtar Baraket*."

And so, *effendi*, there passed out of my life, Mariam, a pearl of great price, a jewel among a million. And though Allah might vouchsafe me a thousand lifetimes, I could never forget her—never cease to love her.

Ho, Silat! Bring the sweet and take the full.

In the sight of Allah, who knows not death, slaying is no great matter; but it is a great matter in the sight of men, who behold death as the end of life.

—*Kasida of El Guri.*

THE DRAGOMAN'S CONFESSION

1

The Wailing Wall of the Jews, *effendi*, is best seen when the shadows begin to lengthen, and not in this midday heat. Yet if you insist——No? Well then, here is the coffee shop of Silat, master brewer of *quahwah*, and I have bethought me of a wondrous adventure of mine, which I never before have related to mortal man.

Is not this shade refreshing after the heat and dust of the street, and is it not better far to be seated on this cushioned *diwan* than tramping beneath the blazing sun?

Ho, Silat! Bring two *narghiles*, heaped with your finest Persian tobacco, and scented with essence of orange flowers. And prepare for us coffee, black as the heel of an Abyssinian eunuch, bitter as aloes and quinine, and hot as the pitch in the cauldron of Jan ibn Jan, Sultan of all evil *jinn*.

The tale, *effendi*, is one which I would hesitate to tell to any but you, a confession of an indiscretion of the days of my youth, when—Allah forgive me!—I transgressed the law of the Koran. It is a story which I should not like to repeat to one who, like myself, is of the Faithful. But you, who have an understanding heart, and a sympathy for all races and creeds, will understand.

Once I told you a tale of a rose, *effendi*—of Selma, beauteous Rose of Mosul. I will now relate to you a story of a lily, a tiger lily from far Cathay. Was it not Sayyidna Isa himself who said that even the glory of the great Suleiman Baalshem, Lord of the Name, was as nothing compared to the splendor of the lily? Consider, then, the golden beauty of the tiger lily, with its slender throat and its graceful curves, greater than that of all other lilies. Reflect on this, *effendi*, and you may be vouchsafed some slight conception of the glorious perfection of a slender, black-eyed maiden of Cathay, who rightfully bore the name, Tiger Lily.

I pray you, *effendi*, for the purpose of this story, think not of me as the bent and wrinkled graybeard who sits before you, but as I looked in the days of my youth—tall and straight as a young pine, strong and brave as a tiger, and handsome as the bright moon of Ramazan.

I have told you, *effendi*, of my great love for Selma Hanoum, and of the magnificent palace we maintained in Mosul. So deep was our affection, each for the other, that it seemed that she but lived to please me, and I, her.

One day as I was strolling through the *souk*, I passed the hidden slave mart where I had purchased Selma in defiance of the Pasha's eunuch. It brought back a flood of memories, so, recalling the password, I made my way through the shop of the rug vender, which veiled the courtyard where this secret traffic was conducted.

* * * *

I saw that I had arrived late, as most of the business of the day had been transacted. Many buyers were about to depart with their purchases, young and old, male and female, white, yellow, brown and black. But one slave remained to be sold, a young maid of Cathay. Her master, a gray-bearded Pathan, helped her to mount the platform, and stood by while the auctioneer lifted the concealing cloak from her shapely shoulders, the better to display her charms to prospective purchasers.

"Ho, Defenders of the Faith," he cried. "Behold! Praise God for permitting your eyes to see this lovely flower from far Cathay. Lo Foo Goak, the Tiger Lily, a princess in her own right, only daughter of a great Chinese war-lord. Worth her weight in gold. What am I offered?"

A beetle-browed Kurd at my left bid fifty piasters, which was, of course, only meant to start the bidding, as her master would scarcely have parted with a paring of her nail for so low a price.

The girl was undeniably beautiful by any standard. There was just enough tilt to her heavy-lidded almond eyes to give here a piquant expression. Her nose was small and straight, and her lips were twin rose-petals of delight. The clinging, translucent silk of her Chinese costume revealed firm, virginal breasts, a slender waist, and limbs that were marvels of grace and perfection.

The bidding swiftly grew louder and the bidders more clamorous as they began to realize, one after another, the tremendous worth of the slave-girl who stood before them. Of course, none believed that she was a princess, any more than did I, who knew the extravagant lengths to which auctioneers would go to dispose of their merchandise. But all knew the great market value of such unusual grace and beauty.

I stood idly looking on, taking no great interest in the proceedings, when the thought occurred to me that Selma Hanoum would be pleased with the gift of such a slave-girl. I took inventory of my gold, and found that I had about seventy pounds Turkish. The bidding had, by that time, reached fifty pounds, or five thousand piasters.

"I am bid but five thousand piasters for this Virgin of Paradise, this daughter of a Chinese prince, stolen from the garden of her father's palace by a Mongol raider, and sold by him to Yusuf ben Ali, the Pathan merchant prince, for a lakh of rupees. If a single para less than that sum is bid, he will take her to Samarkand, where beauty such as hers is appreciated."

The bidders had, by this time, narrowed down to two, a wrinkled *shaykh*, and a blubber-lipped Moor, black as ebony and ugly as a baboon. With much squabbling back and forth, they were raising each other's bids, ten piasters at a time.

"Six thousand piasters," I said.

Both stared at me, as if disgusted with my lack of business acumen, but the auctioneer fairly beamed.

"Six thousand piasters," he cried. "Who will bid seven?"

The *Magrhebi* raised my bid another ten piasters, and the *shaykh* raised his bid another ten. I grew impatient of their haggling.

"Seven thousand," I cried.

The two bidders glared at me, then looked sympathetically at each other.

"By Allah! Such bidding is outlandish," muttered the *Magrhebi*.

"*Ayewah!* It is ruinous," agreed the *shaykh*. "I am through."

"Not I," announced the *Magrbebi*. Then he shouted: "Seven thousand and ten piasters."

Hastily I rechecked the contents of my purse. This was more money than I had with me.

"I am bid seven thousand and ten piasters," cried the auctioneer. "Who will raise the bid?"

I shrugged my shoulders, and turned away. Then I heard a cry from the girl, which caused me to look back. She had drawn a knife from beneath her garments, and now held it poised above her bosom. "Dare to sell me to that filthy Blackamoor, O Pathan," she cried, "and I will slay myself."

The *Magrhebi* grinned. "*Waha!*" he exclaimed. "She is a little tigress. But fear not, O Pathan, I can tame her." In his hand he held a heavy, three-lashed *kurbaj* of twisted rhinoceros hide. With the quickness of a darting serpent, he struck, and the knife flew from the girl's fingers and tinkled on the flagstones of the courtyard.

"Seven thousand and ten," intoned the auctioneer. "Who will bid eight thousand?"

Again the *Magrhebi* grinned, and looked about him. Then he said: "There are no more bidders, auctioneer. She is mine. And here is your gold." He tossed a bag onto the platform, and reached up to help the girl down. But she drew back from him. "I will not be slave of yours, O great African ape," she said, defiantly.

With a frown, the *Magrhebi* swung his *kurbaj* and flicked her bare shoulder, raising three red welts. "Come quickly," he commanded, "or my three little black snakes will bite harder, and the next time they will draw blood."

"Never!"

He drew back his whip for a blow, but the girl did not flinch. She regarded him with a look of haughty disdain.

Again he swung the *kurbaj*. But by that time I had come up to him. Before he could lash her a second time I wrenched the whip from his grasp.

He turned to me, an evil look in his eyes, and laid his hand on his simitar. "So, my young cockerel, you would interfere between a man and his slave. Give me back my whip."

"Here it is," I replied, and lashed him across the face.

He whipped out his simitar, at this, but I brought the heavy butt of the whip down on his wrist, so numbing it that the weapon dropped from his fingers. Then I jerked his bag of gold from the hands of the astonished auctioneer, and hurled it into the *Magrhebi's* midriff with such force that he doubled up and fell on his face, while the coins from the bursted bag rolled all about him.

"Now take your gold, and get out," I told him, "or your three little black snakes shall sup on the blood of their master."

* * * *

Half dazed, and completely cowed, he got to his knees and whined: "Do not whip me, master. I but jested, my lord. I would not have struck the girl again."

I tossed the whip to him, and turned to confront the astounded auctioneer, and the enraged Yusuf ben Ali, the girl's Pathan master.

"By God and again by God!" raged the Pathan. "How dare you ruin my business? I will go before the Pasha. I will have you beaten with palm rods. You—"

"Enough, *sidi*," I interrupted. "I will pay you eight thousand piasters for the girl. Does that suffice you?"

"Money talks," he replied. "Let me see your gold."

"Here are seven thousand piasters," I said, tossing him my purse. "Count them. And here," drawing a blazing ruby from my finger, "is a ring worth twenty thousand. I will leave it with our friend the auctioneer as surety, and he will pay you the other thousand."

The auctioneer examined the ring, a present to me from Selma Hanoum which I valued very highly, and with which I would not have consented to part permanently for any sum. Yusuf ben Ali counted the gold over twice. "It is correct," he said, finally.

"I will pay you the other thousand and keep the ring as surety," the auctioneer told him.

"I'll call for the ring this afternoon," I said. "Have it ready for me."

I helped the girl down from the platform. Then she adjusted her cloak and veil and we walked out, passing the blubber-lipped *Magrhebi* as he crawled about on his hands and knees, muttering to himself and retrieving his gold, past the staring crowd of purchasers and slaves, through the shop of the rug merchant, and into the street.

I swiftly led the way to the palace of Selma Hanoum, hoping she would be pleased with this beautiful gift I had brought her, and anxious to see the look on her face when I should unveil the gorgeous slave-girl from Cathay.

But as soon as I entered the *salamlik*, I knew that something was wrong. The *bowab* was not at the door, and in the rooms beyond I heard the women keening.

Completely forgetting the little slave-girl, I rushed into the *majlis*. There on a *diwan* lay my beautiful Selma, her women wailing around her.

In an instant I was at her side. On her face was the pallor of death, and there hovered about her the faint odor of crushed peach kernels.

"Selma!" I cried. "Selma, beloved!"

I touched her brow. It was cold as marble.

"She has been received into the mercy of Allah, *sidi*," sobbed one of her women.

2

I knelt there beside the mortal remains of my beloved, too stunned with grief to know or care what went on around me. Presently, however, I became aware that some one was speaking to me. It was the little stave-girl I had just purchased. She had taken a small piece of pastry from a tray that stood on a near-by taboret, and was holding it before me.

"Do you recognize this odor, master?" she asked.

I sniffed it. "Bitter almonds. Cherry laurel," I said. "What does it matter?" Having once been an *attar*, I recognized the familiar odor of a common flavoring essence.

"Might it not also be poison—prussic acid?" she asked.

True. Blinded by my grief, I had not even thought of this. It must be poison, for Selma had evidently been in perfect health when I had left her a few hours before.

I got to my feet. "Who brought these pastries to the mistress?" I asked.

An old slave-woman answered. "I brought them, *sidi*."

"And where did you get them?"

"The new cook made them, my lord."

The new cook! This brought suspicions. The day before, our old cook and his helper had left us to take employment with Ahmed Aga, one of the most prosperous of the dignitaries of Mosul, who had offered them ridiculously high wages. Shortly thereafter, two other men who had applied for their positions had been employed. I had not liked the looks of either of them at the time, but Selma had taken them on trial.

"Where is Musa, the eunuch?" I asked.

"Here, my lord." Musa parted the hangings of the rear door of the *majlis*, and stepped within the room.

"Bring the new cook and his helper into the *salamlik*," I commanded.

"Harkening and obedience, *sidi*."

I went into the *salamlik*. Presently Musa entered with the new cook, a short, rotund, greasy-faced *Turki* named Sufeyd.

"Where is your helper?" I asked.

"He has gone to the *souk, sidi*," replied Sufeyd, "to buy meat and vegetables."

"So? Who made the pastry that was served to your mistress today?"

"I made it, my lord."

"And what strange flavor did you add to it?"

"I added naught but essence of almonds," he replied, sullenly. "My helper obtained it for me. He told me a few drops in the fill-ing of each cake would give them a delicious flavor, thus pleasing my mistress with my work."

"Here is the essence, *sidi*," said Musa. He drew a small phial from his clothing and handed it to me. I drew the cork, and a whiff convinced me that it was indeed prussic acid.

"So your helper gave you this poison," I said. "A likely story, yours. A cook taking advice from his helper."

"Poison! *Sidi*, I swear to you by my head and beard, by the tombs of my forefathers, that I knew it not. *Sidi*, have mer—"

He got no further. Blinded by grief and rage, and thoroughly disbelieving the story of this villainous-looking rascal, I had whipped out my simitar. A swift, sure blow, and his head flew from his shoulders, cutting off his speech for ever.

A moment later, I repented my rash act, when repentance came too late. I reflected that Sufeyd might have been telling the truth after all, that he might have been the dupe of some one else. But, assuming that he had not used the poison innocently, thinking it a harmless flavoring essence, and had been in a plot with others, I had for ever sealed the only lips which could tell me who those others might be.

As I stood there thus, with the poison phial in one hand and the bloody simitar in the other, the front door was suddenly flung open, and Daoud Aga, the *Yuzbashi*, or Captain of the *Hytas*, the Turkish Irregular Cavalry, entered, followed by a file of soldiers.

"Hah!" he cried. "I am sent to arrest you for one murder, and find that you have committed two. By slaying your accomplice you have saved the headsman one stroke, but he shall not be cheated of the other."

"What do you mean? Who sent you?" I asked.

"I mean that you are under arrest for having ordered the poisoning of your wife, Selma Hanoum. His Excellency the Pasha sent me. If you have any further questions, let them wait until you stand before His Excellency."

3

Hafiz Pasha, supreme ruler of the Pashalik of Mosul, glared at me as I was brought before him. I could see that, in his mind, I was convicted before being tried. Beside him sat Ahmed Aga, the man who had hired our cook and helper the day before. He was a handsome and extremely vain fellow of about my own age, and affected a short, crisply curled black beard.

"O miserable and ungrateful wretch of a *Badawi*," said the Pasha. "Dare you deny the heinous crime of which you have been accused?"

"I have not been faced with an accuser, as yet, Your Excellency," I reminded him.

"You will face him soon enough!" He turned to a soldier. "Bring the witness," he commanded.

Ahmed Aga stroked his tightly curled beard and smiled.

"May it please Your Excellency, we have evidence enough to convict him without the witness," said Daoud Aga. "Before I could arrest him, the villain had committed a second murder. Here is the poison phial, and here the bloody simitar with which he slew his accomplice, the cook." He laid the two articles before the Pasha.

"So, O spawn of a pestilence, you sought to cover your trail with blood!"

"I sought vengeance, Excellency, on the slayer of my wife. In the extremity of my anger and grief, I—"

"Enough, O father of lies! Here is the witness."

The soldier, at this moment, ushered into the room Mustafa, the shifty-eyed young *Turki* who had been employed to act as the deceased cook's assistant.

"Tell your tale, Mustafa, and have no fear of your master," said the Pasha.

"I bear witness," said the fellow, looking down his greasy nose and avoiding my gaze, "that my master gave a bottle of strong-smelling essence to Sufeyd, the cook, this morning, and ordered him to use it in flavoring the pastries he was to prepare for my mistress."

"You lie, O scum of the gutters!" I cried, springing toward him.

He cringed back, guilty fear written on his face. But the soldiers gripped me and dragged me back.

I appealed to the Pasha. "Your Excellency, would you condemn an innocent man on the unsupported word of so low a scoundrel?"

"It happens, O vile poisoner and assassin," replied the Pasha, "that his word is not unsupported." He signed to a soldier. "Bring the other witnesses."

* * * *

Two more ruffians of the type who would whine for a para by day, and slit your throat for one at night, were ushered in. They stated that they were friends of Sufeyd, and that they had stopped in his kitchen to pass the time of day with him that morning. Then both subscribed to the falsehood that while there, they had seen me give the powerful essence to the cook, with instructions to use it in the pastry he was preparing for the *hanoum*.

"What have you to say to this, O double murderer?" asked the Pasha, when they had finished.

"That I have never seen these lying malefactors before. For reasons best known to themselves, they bear false witness, as did the other."

"Perhaps you have a witness to prove that you were not in the kitchen this morning?"

"As a matter of fact, I was in the kitchen this morning," I replied.

"Hah!"

"But Selma Hanoum was with me. I stood beside her while she hired Sufeyd and this lying villain, Mustafa."

"And you did not return later, as these three witnesses have testified?"

"No."

"Since you show no signs of repentance and confession, I will confront you with still further evidence of your guilt." He motioned to a soldier, who went out, and returned with an old Jew, whom I recognized as the keeper of a small chemist shop in the *souk*.

"Ishak," said the Pasha, pointing to me, "have you ever seen this person before?"

"Often, Your Excellency," replied the chemist. "Only this morning he purchased from me a small phial of prussic acid."

"Ah! Is this the phial?"

"It is the same, Your Excellency."

"That is all. The witnesses may go."

As the four false witnesses who had sworn away my life filed out, I bowed my head to await my sentence. After all, what did it matter if death should claim me now? With the passing of Selma Hanoum, the light of my life had gone out. Why, then, should I cling to the empty shell of existence that remained? But life is sweet to us all, no matter how barren or sordid it may be, and so I spoke again to the Pasha.

"These are lies, all lies. Some one has poisoned my wife and conspired to ruin me—has paid these cutthroat dregs of Mosul to bear false witness. What possible reason could I have to slay her whom I loved above all else in the world?"

"That, O double murderer, we can answer, also," replied the Pasha. He turned to Ahmed Aga. "Produce your papers, *sidi*."

The *aga* drew from beneath his cloak a paper, the edges of which were brown and cracked with age, and respectfully handed it to the Pasha.

"Here, O dog of a *Badawi*, is a document signed by Ali Pasha, father of Selma Hanoum—may Allah concede them both mercy!—in which he acknowledges the receipt from the father of Ahmed Aga, on whom be peace, of twenty thousand pounds. I have had the interest computed, and the total amount now due is forty-two thousand pounds.

"Selma Hanoum knew of the existence of this note, but the noble and generous Ahmed Aga, because of the friendship which had always existed between their fathers, never pressed her for payment, knowing that she, the greatest lady of Mosul, would thereby be impoverished, and hoping that she would marry some one with wealth and station to match her own, so that this considerable part of his inheritance might be returned to him.

"But she wedded with him, O consort of mangy camels—with a penniless beggar from the desert wastes. Without a doubt, she told you of the debt, and you plotted to elude it and seize her wealth by compassing her death and becoming her heir, knowing that the obligation of her father could not be brought to you for payment. You asked for a reason, and I have the reason here, signed and sealed by Ali Pasha, two witnesses, and a venerable *kazi*."

"Your Excellency," I cried, aghast at the net of false evidence which was tightening around me, "that paper is a forgery, and the man who forged it sits in the place of honor at your right hand. I see it all, now. It was Ahmed Aga who hired my cook and helper and sent his own tools to apply for their places, Ahmed Aga whose gold paid these dregs of the bazars to bear false witness against me, in order that he might seize the palace and property of Selma Hanoum."

The Pasha looked horrified. Then his brows knitted in anger. "Vile wretch and base prevaricator!" he said, "think not to avert your fate by maligning one of our most pious and upright citizens. For such as you, any death is too good. Had you shown some sign of repentance I would only have had you beheaded, but as it is, you shall have a more lingering and painful passing." He turned to Daoud Aga. "Take this low-born swine to the center of the *souk*, and there impale him, that all may see his shameful death, and that other villains of his stripe may be warned."

Once more Ahmed Aga smiled, as he stroked his curled black beard.

4

As the soldiers dragged me from the Pasha's presence, I saw, standing near the door, a slight veiled figure. For a moment, a pair of night-black almond eyes gazed into mine and flashed me a look of sympathy which showed that among those who stood in the audience chamber, I had at least one friend. I recognized my little slave-girl from Cathay.

The thought came that I should at least give this girl her freedom before being done to death, but when I held back to speak to her, my conductors jerked me forward, while Daoud Aga, walking behind, prodded me with the point of his simitar.

A crowd of riffraff which had gathered in the street outside, greeted me with cries of: "Kill the poisoner! Slay the assassin!" and many coarse jests at my expense. "Where is he to be beheaded?" I heard one ask, as the rabble fell in around and behind me.

"He is not to be beheaded," answered a soldier, "but will be permitted to view the *souk* from a lofty and narrow seat until such time as Shaitan shall see fit to seize upon his condemned soul."

"An impalement!" cried another. "How long will he live, *effendi*?"

"Only Allah is all-knowing, *ya hu*," replied the soldier; "yet if his viscera be sufficiently tough he may last out the day, and even glimpse tomorrow's sun."

Dazed by the terrible realization of what was in store for me, I stumbled on, scarce hearing their foul jests and fouler maledictions. Those who could get near enough, kicked, struck, pinched and pulled me, while others hurled refuse and spat upon me. Soon my garments hung in filthy tatters and my body was a mass of bruises. I could scarcely realize that I, an innocent man, and until now one of the most affluent and respected citizens of the pashalik, was about to suffer the death by torment which is meted out only to the lowest and most depraved felons. It seemed that I must be the victim of some hideous nightmare from which I would presently waken—that these, my tormenters, did not really mean to slay me.

By the time I reached the *souk*, I was so weakened by the beating I had received and the contemplation of the horrible fate that was planned for me, that I could scarcely stand, but was supported on either side by the two soldiers.

Presently the executioner came, pushing his way through the crowd and carrying a heavy stake on one shoulder. An assistant followed him with a spade. The executioner drew his *jambiyah* and began whittling the narrow end of the stake, while his helper commenced the heavier but less skilful task of digging the hole for it.

Evidently an expert in his line, the executioner took great pride in his grim profession. The conscious cynosure of all eyes, he worked with many flourishes and grandiose gestures, yet with extreme care in order that the stake might have just the proper degree of sharpness and smoothness to insure me a lingering and painful death. For if it were too sharp, my weight might instantly drive it into my vitals and thus swiftly release me from my misery, while a few rough edges or splinters might cause hemorrhages which would lead to coma and death, thus again defeating his purpose, and disappointing the crowd which counted on gloating over my miseries for many hours to come.

His whittling done with, the executioner critically surveyed the work of his perspiring assistant, who was just completing the hole. After a few unnecessary instructions, which were obviously intended to parade his authority before the rabble rather than instruct his helper, he took a cord from beneath his garments, and ordered me to hold out my wrists to be bound.

At this juncture, however, there occurred a sudden interruption. "Make way for the Pasha's emissary," some one shouted. "Stand aside for the messenger of His Excellency."

There was a clatter of hoofbeats behind me, and a rider, whose features I could not see because a corner of the *kufiyah* was drawn across the face, clattered up, waving a pistol menacingly, and crying: "By order of the Pasha, this execution must stop. The prisoner is to be taken before His Excellency at once, as new evidence has just come to light. Set the prisoner on the horse."

Daoud Aga looked insolently up at the rider. "Whence came you, fool?" he asked. "Be off, before we sharpen a second stake for you."

"I am from the Pasha, O great baboon," replied the rider, pointing the pistol full at the Captain's head. "Order the prisoner placed on the horse at once, or this instant will I send your unbelieving soul to Eblis, who waits to seize it."

Daoud Aga quite evidently did not believe that the rider was from the Pasha. Nor, for that matter, did I. The Captain seemed convinced, however, that the daring horseman meant business, for his face paled, and he signed to the two soldiers to lift me into the saddle. They complied, for I was too weak to mount alone. I swayed dizzily, and would have fallen but for my tight grip on the pommel. A swift glance at me evidently convinced the rider that I could hang on, for we wheeled and rode off through the disappointed crowd in the direction of the Pasha's palace.

* * * *

Before we had ridden far, I heard the report of firearms behind us, and bullets began singing around our heads. My rescuer, who was still leading my horse, suddenly turned toward the east gate of the city. We passed through the gate unchallenged, clattering across a stone bridge, then a narrow island, then a bridge of boats—for the Tigris was at flood and the ford impassable—and landing, plunged through the dust and desolation that had once been mighty Nineveh. Presently we turned again, this time toward the northwest, following the windings of the river, so I judged that we were making for Telkef.

After we had ridden thus at breakneck speed for some ten miles, we stopped to breathe our horses. During that swift ride my companion had not addressed a word to me, and I had been too weak to attempt any conversation. I had noticed that my rescuer was small, much smaller than the average man, but I gasped in amazement when, with the *kufiyah* drawn aside, I recognized my little slave-girl.

"Lo Foo!" I exclaimed. "So it was you who saved my life! May Allah requite you."

"To abandon one's master is to become a flower without a root," she replied, modestly. "Here, I have brought you a simitar, *jambiyah* and pistol."

She handed me a bundle, which I unwrapped. The wrapper was a cloak and contained the weapons she had named. I armed myself as she was armed, and threw the cloak over my tattered garments.

"By what powerful magic did you obtain these horses, weapons and clothing?" I asked.

"Fowls are best caught with rice grains," she replied. "I saw two *Hytas* who had just ridden into the city, standing beside their horses. To one, I signed with the eyes as I passed. Then I turned into an empty dwelling near by, but as I turned, I signed also to the other, unknown to the first.

"When the first seized me, I snatched his pistol and held him off, whereupon the second came to my rescue. They quarreled, and the second man choked the first into unconsciousness. Then, with the butt of the pistol, I sent him to join his fellow in oblivion. It was easy to appropriate what clothing and weapons I needed, and ride off with the horses."

"You are a jewel of inestimable worth, Lo Foo," I said, "and have performed a dangerous and difficult task as no man could have accomplished it."

"No jewel sparkles except by reflected light, my lord," she replied. "If I have attained some brilliance, it is in the light of your presence. But come. You are weary and wounded. If I mistake not, that is a deserted farmer's hut at the foot of yonder hill, and there are provisions in the saddle-bags."

"Tiger Lily," I said, as we walked our horses toward the tumbledown hut, "I am a broken and ruined man, a fugitive from the power of the Pasha, yet you honor me as if I were a sultan, with all the wealth and magnificence of Salah ad Din."

For some time she made no answer. Then, as she turned her face toward me, I saw that tears trembled on her long, curved lashes. "I am a stranger in a strange land," she replied. "You saved me from worse than death at the hands of that black, blubber-lipped *Shaitan*. You are my master—my father and my mother. Shall I, who would have shared your prosperity, desert you in adversity?"

"You have read me a lesson in loyalty which I shall never forget," I told her.

5

As no signs of pursuit developed, we permitted our tired horses to walk all the way to the hut. Then we tethered them, and went inside. I gathered wood and soon had a fire crackling, while Lo Foo brought a waterskin and a few utensils, some flour, sugar, dates, clarified butter, and coffee, which she had found in the saddle-bags. First she set the dates to simmering in the clarified butter. Then she mixed bread. While it was baking, she brewed coffee.

Watching her make these preparations, I marveled at the wondrous ways in which Allah guides our footsteps so that we may fulfil our destinies. Had I not idly wandered into the slave mart that morning, and then been led to purchase this slave-girl for Selma Hanoum, I would have been, at that very moment, dying a slow and painful death, hooted and jeered by the rabble of Mosul.

We sipped coffee until the food was ready, then ate our dates and freshly baked bread. Our simple meal finished, Lo Foo brewed more coffee, then pleasantly surprized me with a *chibouk*, which she had found in the saddle-bag, stuffed with *Suryani* tobacco and surmounted by a glowing coal from the fire.

Although Lo Foo was bright and cheerful, and was obviously trying to distract my mind from the great sorrow which had overtaken me, my bosom was constricted and I had not the power of peace. Presently, as I grew more melancholy with each thought of my lost Selma, I arose, and went outside to attend to our horses. After unsaddling the weary beasts and rubbing them with grass, I took them down to the river, about a half-mile distant, to drink.

The sun had dropped low on the horizon, so I made ablution and prayed the sunset prayer, ere I started back. I was walking toward the hut in the gathering dusk, leading the horses, when six armed men, who had evidently been watching me from ambush, suddenly sprang out of a ravine only a short distance from the hut, and confronted me. The foremost, whom I recognized as one of the cutthroats who had home false witness against me, plucked out a pistol and snapped it in my face. It did not go off, luckily for me, and drawing my own pistol, I shot him through the heart.

As he slumped to the ground, another fired at me and missed. In the meantime, the four remaining villains, who had no pistols, had drawn their simitars, and began to circle me to the right and left. The horses had not flinched during the shooting, and now, seeing that against such overwhelming odds my only hope lay in flight, I turned and swung to the bare back of my mount, and slapped him on the flank.

The well-trained beast responded with a leap and a burst of speed that quickly took me out of reach of my assailants, while his mate galloped behind me. But it was written that I should not thus escape them, for the animal suddenly stumbled and went to his knees, pitching me over his head. I fell heavily, alighting on my back with such force that the wind was knocked from me. For a few moments I lay there, gasping for breath and unable to rise. I could hear the triumphant cries of my enemies and the thudding of their feet as they came nearer and nearer, which stimulated me to make desperate efforts to get to my feet. Finally I succeeded, and drawing my simitar and *jambiyah*, stood there at bay, reeling like a man whose senses have been stolen by *arak*.

Seeing the plight I was in, my enemies advanced with exultant shouts. One, whom I recognized as the third miscreant to bear false witness against me before the Pasha, sprang in close, expecting to find me an easy victim, and slashed viciously at my neck. He proved to be a clumsy swordsman, and weak as I was, I managed to parry the blow and return one in kind, which stretched him on the ground.

This gave the others pause, and for a moment they stood back, shouting curses at me. It was evident that whoever they might be, they were neither swordsmen nor soldiers, so I judged that, like the two I had slain, they must be hirelings of Ahmed Aga. The one who had a pistol began to reload it, so I did the same with mine. Seeing this, he desisted, and called to his companions to all charge me at once.

By this time I had recovered my breath, and my confidence in myself had been considerably heightened. I thrust the still useless pistol back into my sash, and once more drew simitar and *jambiyah*. They spread out to surround me, but still feared to come within reach of my blade. Lying scattered on the ground in the vicinity were a number of ancient bricks, made before the time of Suleiman ben Daoud, on whom be peace, and stamped with cuneiform inscriptions. They had evidently fallen from the panniers of some pilferer of the ruins of Nineveh, perhaps during a raid by robbers, who naturally would not carry off such things. My cowardly assailants now began hurling these bricks at me, and as they kept coming from several directions at once, I could not avoid them all, dodge as I would. Presently, after I had received a number of painful, though not dangerous bruises, one struck my left knee, so paralyzing it that I was forced to stand on my right leg only. A moment later, another caught me on the back of the head, and down I went, still dimly conscious, but unable to move hand or foot.

With yells of triumph, my enemies now rushed in to finish me. One planted his foot on my body, and raised his simitar to hack off my head. I was convinced that my end had come.

But at that moment a pistol shot rang out, and my would-be beheader fell across my body, blood oozing from a round hole in his forehead. Then Lo Foo, who had been attracted by the sounds of the conflict, came running up. She threw down her smoking pistol, and drawing her simitar with her right hand, snatched mine up with her left.

What came after took place so swiftly that my eyes, dulled by the blow I had received, could scarcely follow. Often had I seen men fight with simitar and *jambiyah*, but never before had I seen any one use *two* simitars at the same time. She struck at the head of my nearest enemy with the right, and when he parried, brought the left across his abdomen with a swift, drawing cut, disemboweling him.

The remaining two had, meanwhile, recovered from their astonishment at this sudden onslaught, and as their comrade went down, both attacked her simultaneously. I have said that these men were obviously not expert swordsmen, and that was true enough; yet with two of them against one, and that one a mere slip of a girl, I despaired for her life. I made a desperate effort to rise, and succeeded in dragging myself from beneath the body that had fallen across me. But when I tried to get to my feet, a dizziness assailed me, and I fell back to my elbows.

Through the dim haze that had gathered before my eyes, I saw a bewildering whirl of swiftly flying blades. Then suddenly one of Lo Foo's antagonists went down with his head split open. The other, seeing his comrade's fate, turned to flee, but only hastened his own end. The girl sprang forward, and with a sweeping moulinet smote his neck so that his head leaped from his shoulders. After that I saw no more, for consciousness left me, and it seemed that I was sinking into a black, cold void.

6

When my senses returned, it was broad daylight. I was lying in the hut, with two cloaks beneath me, and two more thrown over me. A pile of pistols, simitars and *jambiyahs* lay on the floor, and beyond them, eight saddles, with saddle-bags, waterskins and other equipment, were piled against the wall.

I sat up, and discovered at one and the same time a dull ache in my head and a sharp pain in my left knee. Exploration revealed a bump on the back of my head that had been carefully bound. Raising my coverings, I saw that my knee, also, had been bandaged. Then Lo Foo entered.

Depositing the bundle of firewood she was carrying beside the smoldering fire, she came over, and kneeling beside me, said: "Good morning, my lord. I trust that you slept well, and that the pain of your injuries has grown less."

"I rested in complete oblivion, little one," I replied, "and the wounds are nothing. But tell me, who brought me here, and whence came all these weapons and this equipment?"

"I brought you, my lord."

"You brought me!"

"Yes, master."

"But how?"

"I carried you."

"*Wallah!* You carried me?" I looked at her slight figure, her slender limbs and dainty hands. She was at least a foot shorter than I, and probably did not weigh much more than half as much.

She saw my look of unbelief, and said: "You doubt it? We have a saying: 'The sea is not measured by a bushel, nor is a man always known by his looks.' I will show you."

Before I was aware of what she was about, she had bent and clasped me around the waist. With no more effort than if I had been a sack of grain, she threw me across her shoulder and stood erect. She walked over, and gently lowered me to a place beside the fire, with a little chuckle of merriment. "You see?"

"*Alhamdoliliah!* You are as strong as a man!" I exclaimed.

"Stronger than some men, my lord, but not quite so strong as you," she answered modestly, "though I may understand the laws of leverage better, having been taught them by my father."

"Your father must be a remarkable man," I told her. "Who is he?"

"My father is the Wong Tse, Chin Wah, a prince of the ancient blood, whose lands are partly in China and partly in Mongolia. In the days of his youth, he wandered much in foreign lands. And everywhere he went, he studied methods of offense and defense, both with weapons and with the bare hands, for he knew that some day he must take over the domain of the great warrior prince who was his father, and that it would require a strong man, well versed in these things, to hold that domain."

"Then you are really a princess!" I exclaimed.

"I was once a princess," she corrected. "Now I am but a slave."

"Is it customary in your country to train a princess in the arts of war?" I asked.

"Not at all," she replied. "My father longed for a son. But I was his first-born, and when I came, my mother died. So great was his love for my mother, that when she was taken, he could bear to have no other woman near him. He said that I should be both son and daughter to him, and that when he was gone, I should be war-lord in his place. Accordingly, although he saw that I was educated in all the arts and wiles that are taught our women, he himself, when I was very young, set about teaching me to shoot, fence, box, ride and use the lance. He taught me an art he had learned in Nippon, *jiu jitsu*, and trained me daily in the exercise which he loved best—two-sword fighting.

"As soon as I was old enough, I went with him on hunting expeditions. Once, when we were on a hunt, I became separated from the rest of the party, and was captured by a band of Mongol outlaws, but not before I had slain five of their number and wounded several more.

"The bandit chieftain tried to woo me, but I broke his arm. He would have slain me, then, but his men restrained him. Some called me Lo Foo, the Tigress. My own name, in our language, meant 'Lily.' Soon they were calling me the Tiger Lily. A few days later, the well-guarded caravan of Yusuf ben Ali, the Pathan trader, camped near us, and I was sold to him as the Tiger Lily.

"Yusuf, the old dotard, had me brought to his tent that night. He attempted to beguile me with honeyed phrases, but when he saw that I would have none of him, attempted force. I spared his old bones, but after I had thrown him over my head, he desisted. Later he brought me to Mosul along with other merchandise, having heard that high prices were paid for virgins in its slave market."

* * * *

She had knelt by the fire as she began her narrative, and set about preparing our morning meal, a repetition of the one we had eaten the night before. She looked so gentle, so feminine and so daintily alluring at this domestic task, that had I not seen what I had seen with my own eyes, I should have considered her story wholly incredible.

"Lo Foo," I said, as she handed me my coffee, "some day, if Allah grants me life and strength, I will restore you to your father."

She turned her great black eyes full upon me, and in them was a look of tenderness. "You are kind, my master, but I doubt that such happiness lies in my destiny. And we are taught that it is wise to submit to destiny."

"All things are possible to Allah," I replied.

For some time we ate our simple meal in silence. Then Lo Foo said: "This morning as I went for water, I saw twelve troopers of the *Yuz Bashi* riding along the river bank."

"They were looking for me, beyond a doubt," I replied. "Perhaps we had best leave this place, and ride for the mountains."

"As I was gathering firewood, I saw ten more *Hytas* in the other direction," she continued.

"Strange they didn't see our horses!" I mused.

"I tethered them all in the ravine before daybreak," she replied. "The bodies of our enemies I hid in a clump of shrubs. Fortunately, our fire had burned down to a few glowing coals, and there was no smoke to betray us."

"By the life of my head!" I swore, "now I know that you have not slept all night. We remain here, and you shall sleep all day."

"I will sleep if you so command, master," she replied, submissively. But she would not do so until she had put away the food, cleansed the dishes, and brought my *chibouk* topped with a glowing coal. Then she curled up like a kitten, on the couch of cloaks I had just quitted, and fell asleep almost instantly.

When I had finished my smoke, I went to the doorway and stood idly looking out. During the rest of the day, I saw no less than six parties of *Hytas* pass our hiding-place. But none came to look for us in the ruined hut.

* * * *

In the late afternoon I heard the tinkle of camel bells, and saw a large caravan pass down to the river. It was accompanied by much live stock, and many women and children; so I knew it was not a band of traders but a company of the wandering *Badawin*, seeking pasture for their flocks and herds. Soon a miniature town of tents stood on the river bank, and the countryside was dotted with herds attended by the younger boys of the tribe.

I knew it would only be a question of time before our horses should be discovered in the ravine by these young herdsmen, though they might escape detection for the present, as night would soon fall. So I decided that we had best be on the move. Accordingly, I baked bread, made *samb*, and brewed coffee. Then I awakened Lo Foo.

While we ate the hastily prepared meal, I told her of the *Badawin* encampment, and of my resolve to leave as soon as it should be dark enough to hide our movements.

"Have you decided where we will go, master?" she asked.

"Not definitely," I replied. "Perhaps it will be best to ride east, swim our beasts across the Great Zab, and cross the mountains into Persia."

"And then?"

"I don't know," I confessed.

"The Persians are as likely to slay you for your possessions as the Turks," she said. "I know, for I have just come through Persia."

"That is true," I admitted. "But there, at least, I will not have a price on my head."

"What of these *Badawin*?" she asked. "Should they not prove friendly? You are a *Badawi*, are you not?"

"They are of my race," I replied, "but of a tribe unknown to me. However, all *Badawin* in this territory are unfriendly to the *Hytas* because of the depredations of Mohammed Pasha, Hafiz Pasha's predecessor. Nor would the troopers of the *Yuz Bashi* dare to approach their camp, except in considerable force."

"Then you are one with them in your enmity against the Turkish regime, as well as in race. Why not claim protection from their *shaykh*?"

"In that case," I replied, "Hafiz Pasha would offer a reward for me, and I, a stranger in their midst, should be exchanged soon enough for gold."

For some time Lo Foo knit her delicately arched brows in thought. Then she said: "I doubt that we could ride far in any direction, with the *Hytas* swarming over the country in search of us. And as you say, the *Badawin* might be willing to surrender you to the Pasha if tempted with sufficient gold. I believe there is but one thing for us to do."

"And what is that?"

"Ride back to Mosul."

"What! I trust that you have not taken leave of your senses."

"Tell me, master, have you one friend in Mosul whom you can trust?"

"There is one, yes," I replied. "He was absent on a hunting-trip yesterday, or he would have been at my side to defend me."

"Is he a householder?"

"Yes, and greatly respected in the community," I replied. "He is Hasan Aga, uncle of Selma Hanoum."

"Do you think you can convince him of your innocence?"

"I am sure of it."

"Then, my lord, I suggest that we ride back to Mosul on the back of a camel this very night. We have eight horses, with complete equipment, extra weapons, and supplies. The *Badawin* have many camels, and you should easily be able to arrange a trade with their *shaykh*. I will go in my proper raiment, and as your *harim*."

She took her woman's raiment from one of the saddle-bags, and while I smoked my *chibouk* before the door, swiftly donned it. Presently she appeared in the doorway, cloaked, and veiled to the eyes.

"I regret that I must part with my simitars," she said, "but I have two pistols and a *jambiyah* beneath my cloak, and a bundle of simitars will be strapped to my saddle in case of need. Come, let me change your appearance."

I had already exchanged my tattered finery for the best of the clothing she had taken from my assailants, which was poor enough. She now, after taking a small pot of kohl from among her cosmetics, blackened the inner corners of my eyebrows so they appeared to run together, and kohled my eyelids in such a manner that I looked slightly cross-eyed. Then, after she had darkened the day's growth of mustache which had appeared on my upper lip, her mirror convinced me that I should be able to pass even my closest friends, unrecognized.

* * * *

We saddled the horses, loaded the equipment, and started for the encampment, just before sunset. I rode into camp in time to pray the sunset prayer with a group of young men who had just brought in a herd of camels. Then I asked them to direct me to the tent of their *shaykh*.

They led me to a large and capacious tent of black goat hair, before which stood a tall, handsome *Badawin* about forty years of age. After we had exchanged *taslims*, I said; "I am Sa'id bin Ayyub of the Banu Asadin."

"And I am Shaykh Abd er Rahmin, of the Abu Salman," he replied, courteously. "*Bismillah.* Enter in the Name of Allah. This is your tent, and we are your slaves."

The *shaykh* led me into the reception room of his tent, which was crowded with his relatives and followers, and strangers enjoying his hospitality, and also occupied by two favorite mares and a colt. He bade me be seated, and sat with me, in the upper place, divided from the *harim* by a goatskin curtain. Pipes and coffee were brought, and a small boy, who came from the *harim* at a summons from Abd er Rahmin, was sent back with directions that my wife, who waited outside, was to be taken inside and entertained forthwith.

The *shaykh* politely refrained from questioning me, and we talked trivialities for some time. But gradually I got around to that for which I had come, as is customary with our people.

Abd er Rahmin listened sympathetically while I told him of being set upon by six robbers the day before, nor did he show the slightest disbelief when I said I had vanquished them all, single-handed, and appropriated their horses, weapons and equipment. I told him that I had no use for all these horses and weapons, and as my *harim* was weary of traveling on horseback, would like to exchange four horses with their equipment, for a riding-camel with a *shugduf* litter.

"Were the *harami* from Mosul?" he asked.

"I am positive of that," I replied, "because when they rode up to surround me, thinking me an easy prey, I heard one say that they would take my *harim* back to Mosul to sell in the slave mart."

"By Allah, good!" he exclaimed. "Now I know that you do not wish to take any of their horses into Mosul, for fear they might be recognized."

I had told him this because I knew how his people hated the ruffians of Mosul, hoping it would arouse his sympathy, but I now saw that it had, in addition, aroused his cupidity. He knew he had the power to drive a hard bargain, and would make the most of it.

We haggled back and forth over many cups of coffee, and *sharibat*, and several pipes of '*Ajami*, he because he wished to get all he could for his camel and litter, and I because it was the thing to do, and he would have been suspicious had I not done so. But I had come prepared to leave all our horses, and most of our equipment, in exchange for what I wanted, so in the end the bargain was thus concluded.

For some time, savory odors had been issuing from the women's quarters, and now a sheep, roasted whole, and surrounded by boiled rice drenched in clarified butter, was brought in on a huge platter.

"*Bismillah*," pronounced the *shaykh*, placing me at his right hand, while as many as could conveniently do so squatted around the platter. "With health and appetite."

Highly pleased by the bargain he had driven, Abd er Rahmin showered honors and compliments upon me, and fed me choice bits of meat and dripping balls of rice with his own hand.

I grew nervous before the feast was over, as I was anxious about Lo Foo, knowing she would be expected to unveil and remove her cloak in the *harim*, and wondering how she would conceal her pistols and dagger or account for them. I was also extremely impatient, now that our plans had been made and half carried out, to start for Mosul.

But I was compelled to avoid all appearance of haste, and so remained to partake of fruits, sweetmeats, more coffee, and another pipe. By this time, half the evening had slipped away, so I arose to take leave of my host. He sent one of his small sons into the *harim* for Lo Foo, and we walked out to where a boy watched my dearly purchased camel, which was kneeling, laden and waiting.

Lo Foo came out a moment later, and took her place in the *shugduf*. I climbed in on my side of the crude litter, the camel rose, and we were off, followed by the cordial *taslim* of the *shaykh*.

7

As we rode away from the camp in our swaying litter, the countryside was wrapped in a clear, moonless night that was like a spangled, blue-black cloak, with sparkling stars for sequins.

"How did they treat you in the *harim*?" I asked Lo Foo.

"They were very polite," she replied.

"And didn't they question you?"

"Only as to the health of my parents, brothers and sisters, all my paternal and maternal uncles, aunts and cousins, and yours. I managed to hide my weapons under my sash before I removed my cloak. When I unveiled, I think they took me for a Tatar, as I caught some sullen looks among the older women. But I quickly told them I was from Cathay, whereupon all grew cheerful once more. And were you well received by the *shaykh*, my lord?"

"Most cordially," I replied, "and was particularly and singularly honored after he had made certain he was to profit mightily by my visit. But Abd er Rahmin has a good heart, after all. He could have slain me, and taken everything."

"True," she agreed. "He could have taken everything—like Ahmed Aga."

At mention of my deadly enemy, my anger and grief flared up and were like to choke me, as I thought anew of the irreparable loss I had sustained because of the machinations of this thief and murderer.

Lo Foo must have quickly sensed the effect her words had upon me, for she said: "Pray forgive me, my lord. I spoke hastily, and without thought."

"If I could but meet that vilest of vile poisoners, man to man," I said, "I would quickly put an end to his enjoyment of his ill-gotten gains. As for forgiving you, why, that is done already, for any transgression against me, now or in the future. It is written that for the sake of one good action, a hundred evil ones should be forgotten. And this being true, I am indebted to you to the extent of at least a thousand."

"You are generous, my lord. As we rode out of the camp I thought of a plan which, if possible of execution, might bring about the wish you just expressed—to meet your enemy face to face, where none can interrupt."

"A plan? Tell it to me."

"Not now, master. First let me mature it a little more, and also, if it will not wring your heart too much, tell me of the adventures at which you have hinted, which led up to your marrying Selma Hanoum."

Lo Foo, it was obvious, had a remarkable understanding of the workings of the human emotions. Although it was difficult for me to begin my narrative, I found as I got into it, that this was exactly what I wanted to do—to talk to some one about my lost love, and the romantic adventures which had brought us together. I wanted to linger over each wonderful memory and to share it with a sympathetic and appreciative listener. Such I found Lo Foo to be.

And so, while I related the story of our adventures, and enlarged on the beauty, grace and goodness of my dear departed, thus somewhat easing the burden which hung so heavily upon my heart, our patient beast stepped off the long miles; and before I realized it, we were at the bridge of boats which led to the east gate of Mosul.

We crossed this bridge, the island, and the stone bridge beyond without interruption, but were halted at the gate by a gruff soldier, a half-dozen of whose comrades stood near by.

"Who are you, to ride into the city thus unattended at this hour of the night?" he demanded. "And whence came you?"

"I am Sa'id bin Ayyub," I replied. "We left Telkef early this morning, but were entertained all afternoon and half the evening by the *shaykh* of the Abu Salman, hence the lateness of our arrival."

"Saw you aught of two riders on the way, one a tall, beardless youth of about your own size in tattered finery, the other shorter, and wearing the colors of the *Hytas*?"

"We saw many *Hytas*," I replied, "and several bands stopped to question us, but met no riders such as you describe."

"Whither are you bound?"

"To the house of Ahmed Aga, who is the friend of my cousin. Can you direct me?"

When I mentioned the name of the opulent *aga*, the gruff manner of the soldier changed, as if by magic. Politely, he gave me minute directions as to how I could reach the house which had been my own. Then he stepped aside, and we passed into the city.

* * * *

We made straight for the residence of Ahmed Aga, but of course passed it, and stopped before the house of Hasan Aga. After causing the camel to kneel, I dismounted, and knocked loudly on the door. The place was in darkness, showing that the inmates had retired, but presently I heard shuffling footsteps in the *salamlik*, and the voice of Hasan, himself, asking: "Who are you?"

"Your nephew," I replied. "Open quickly, in the name of Almighty Allah."

"I have many nephews," he replied, cautiously.

"I am he who bought the rose, which was stricken by the viper," I replied, reluctant to give my name for fear of being overheard.

At this, I heard the bolt slide back, and knew that Hasan had understood my allusion to Selma Hanoum and the man who had poisoned her. He opened the door a little way, and held up a flickering lantern, by the yellow light of which I saw his gray-bearded, kindly face. But seeing my changed features, he started back, and was about to close the door again when I thrust my foot through the opening.

"I am really Hamed, O uncle, but in disguise," I said. Then he recognized my voice and flung the door wide.

"Who is with you?" he asked, now speaking in a hushed voice.

"A slave-girl I purchased for Selma Hanoum the morning she was murdered," I replied.

"*Bismillah!* Enter, both of you," he invited. "I will bring in your equipment and turn the camel free. It would not do for the beast to be found in my stables. Suspicions might thus be aroused."

Lo Foo and I stepped into the *salamlik*, and waited there in the darkness. Presently I heard him slap the beast's flank and order it to be off. Then he came in with our meager pile of belongings.

"I left the litter on the mangy beast," he said. "Both are so dilapidated that it is problematical which will break down first. But come into the *majlis*. You must be weary and hungry."

"Weary we are, uncle," I replied, "but not hungry, as we have been stuffed by the *shaykh* of the Abu Salman. However, I'll smoke a pipe with you after we find a place for Lo Foo to sleep; that is, if you want to hear my story tonight."

"She shall have my empty *harim*, and welcome," replied Hasan. "As you know, though I have been enabled to keep this house and in a measure refurnish it, due to your generosity and that of my sister's daughter, on whom be Allah's mercy and His blessing, my business has not prospered, and I have been unable either to marry, or purchase slaves. As Ahmed Aga took over all the possessions of Selma Hanoum this morning, and I was assured of no further income from her estate, I was forced to discharge my servants."

He led the way through the scantily furnished *majlis*, into the sitting-room of the *harim*. In this there was but a single *diwan*, one small rug, several ottomans, and a few taborets. Hasan took a candle from a niche, and lighting it, led Lo Foo to the door of one of the sleeping-rooms. He gave her the candle, and said: "In there you may sleep, little one, safe from all fear."

We then returned to the *majlis*, and bidding me be seated, he went out to fetch pipes and coffee. He returned presently, but before he had the charcoal glowing, Lo Foo came out of the *harim*. She was attired in the clinging, silken garments of her native land, which set off her slender beauty, and had donned a thin, translucent face-veil, out of respect to Hasan Aga, though she was no *Moslemah*.

"I slept all day, master," she said to me, "and can not retire so early. Permit me to serve you, and to remain with you for yet a little while."

Without waiting for my reply, she went over and took the coffee things from Hasan, who, nothing loth, turned everything over to her and came and sat beside me. Though he was far gone in years, I saw his eyes kindle with admiration as he glimpsed her thus without her heavy street garments, and knew that the years had not robbed him of his appreciation of beauty.

While we waited for our coffee and *narghiles*, Hasan told me what I most wanted to hear. He described the magnificent funeral of my lost love, and told me where she had been buried. Tears were welling both from his eyes and mine, when Lo Foo served us.

I then related in detail my adventures since my purchase of Lo Foo, and when I had finished he said, "By Allah, there is no doubt that Ahmed Aga is the *afai*, the venomous viper who caused my sister's daughter to be poisoned, and who bribed false witnesses to swear away your life, that he might get possession of her wealth and property. Small wonder that, when he learned of your escape, he set six of his own cutthroats on your trail with orders to slay you. The Pasha must be told the truth of this matter."

"Who is to tell him?" I asked. "And what proof is there? You and I know that Ahmed Aga is guilty, and that I am innocent, but how can we prove it?"

Hasan stroked his white beard. "Aye. That's the difficulty," he said. "We can't. And it would be of no use to go before Hafiz Pasha without proof."

"I know a way to bring the murderer to justice, my lord, and restore to you all but her whom you have lost for ever," said Lo Foo, placing fresh charcoal on my pipe-bowl. "But it will take time."

"To accomplish my purpose, I would spend a lifetime, if need be," I replied. "What is the plan?"

"It will not take a lifetime," she said, "but it will take months."

"And what am I to do in the meantime?" I asked.

"You are to grow a beard," she replied, and turning, retired to her room.

8

Despite the fact that I was confined in the house of Hasan Aga, the months passed quickly. This, I know now, was because of Lo Foo, but at the time I did not realize it. She went out daily in her woman's garb, that concealed all but her eyes, purchasing our food and tobacco in the *souk*, preparing our meals, and looking after our comforts as only a woman can.

One day she brought back four Chinese swords she had purchased, *gims*, she called them, and thereafter, each day, she taught me two-sword fighting as she had learned it from her father, the great war-lord. Often, when I was morose, she danced for me, graceful, rhythmic love-dances, into which she put such depths of feeling that, had I not been blinded by my sorrow and by my hatred of the man who had brought it upon me, would have then revealed her true feeling toward me.

I was not blind to her beauty, but believed I appreciated it as one does a great work of art, unconscious of the flame which, day by day, grew brighter in my bosom.

Often we whiled away the long hours with story-telling. I would relate to her stories I remembered from *The Thousand Nights and a Night*, and she, in turn, would tell me marvelous tales of devils and dragons, of love and war, which she had learned from her own people. Also, she gave me lessons in her language, which I knew passably well because of my previous journey through Cathay, and I taught her to read and write Arabic.

My only other amusement was looking out through the latticed windows of the upper story at the passing throngs of the city. Almost daily I saw the perfidious Ahmed Aga, with his curled beard and magnificent robes, riding forth from, or returning to, the palatial home that had once been mine, on a prancing, richly caparisoned charger. And at such times the hot blood would rush to my face, and my anger and grief would drive me to distraction.

One day I sat before the lattice with Lo Foo beside me, when a procession of strangers such as one seldom sees in Mosul, passed. Brown-skinned, they were, with slanting eyes and high cheek-bones. Their leader, and several of the others, wore ragged, drooping mustaches, but most of them were smooth-faced. They wore queer, funnel-shaped hats with turned-up rims. Some of them had straight, shiny queues hanging down their backs. Their garments were of heavy quilted material edged with fur or wool, and they bestrode sturdy, shaggy ponies, the like of which I had never seen before. All wore swords. Some carried muskets, some bows and arrows, and some, long, slender lances.

I turned to ask Lo Foo if she knew what manner of men they were, and saw that she had gone deadly pale. "Why, what is wrong?" I asked, surprized.

"Those men," she replied, her voice quivering with emotion. "They are a company of my father's Mongol cavalry. And he who rides at their head is Tserin, my father's most trusted captain."

Behind the riders, who numbered at least a hundred, came the cameleers with their stocky, two-humped *Bukhti* camels. They were laden with felt tents, and many bales, bundles and boxes, the contents of which I could only guess. And on several of them rode handsome, richly dressed Chinese girls.

"Your father has sent for you, Lo Foo," I said. "I will have Hasan Aga bring their captain here, and you shall go back with him."

"But master, I—" She hesitated, apparently at a loss for words, her eyes lowered. "I will go, of course, if you wish it. But Tserin must repay you the sum you paid for me."

"You have already repaid me a thousandfold," I replied. "I will not touch your father's gold."

"But what of my plan to help you?" she asked. "It nears fruition. I can not leave you with the task undone."

"I'll accomplish it alone, somehow," I told her.

"No, I will remain to help you. And Tserin shall help us. He can be very useful, as you will see."

* * * *

That afternoon, when Hasan returned, I sent him out to look up the captain of the Mongols. He was to tell him nothing, except that if he would come to his house alone, one would be there who could give him news of her whom he sought.

Lo Foo went into the *harim*, where she spent considerable time, evidently preparing herself to receive her father's captain. For when she emerged, she wore her most gorgeous Chinese raiment, and had done her hair in a strange but exceedingly becoming manner. And she had discarded her veil.

She stopped before me for my approval. "How do you like me thus, master?" she inquired.

"You are gorgeous, as always," I replied. "You are like a precious jewel which blazes forth with undiminished glory in any setting. But I must admit that this one is particularly appropriate."

She smiled, and seated herself on a *diwan*. But the smile was a little wistful, as if I had not said precisely what she wanted to hear.

A moment later, Hasan entered, followed by a stocky Mongol with a long, stringy mustache that drooped at the corners. At sight of Lo Foo unveiled, the *aga* gasped in amazement, but the Mongol dropped to his knees before her and bowed again and again, his forehead touching the floor at each bow.

"This unspeakably base and unworthy person who has the honor of being your slave, rejoices with mighty rejoicing at finding Your Highness alive and well," he said.

Lo Foo smiled, and signed for him to rise: "It is good to see you once more, my faithful Tserin," she replied. "Tell me of my father."

"Alas," said Tserin, "that I should be a bearer of bad tidings! On the day you were stolen from us, the Prince suffered a fall from his horse, which injured his spine. We carried him back to the palace, and the greatest and most skilful of physicians were sent for. They found that his back was broken, and must be put in a cast, if he were to be kept alive, even for a short time. This was done, and they held out hopes for his recovery. But he knew they lied to ease his mental anguish, and demanded the truth. Finally they admitted that he would never ride again, and that he was not long for this earth."

Tears streamed down the old captain's cheeks as he finished his brief recital, and I saw that the eyes of Lo Foo were brimming. But she held up bravely. "You have but confirmed the news which came to me when I saw you at the head of the riders this morning, Tserin," she said, her voice shaking with emotion. "I knew that if my father were alive and able to ride, he would have come for me himself."

"He has sworn to fight off death until you return to take charge of your patrimony," Tserin told her. "Then he will be willing to join his ancestors. I have brought six slave-girls to minister to your wants, and a royal *yurt* with the richest of furnishings, and everything you will require for travel in state. Also, the Prince sent with me much gold, to buy you from him who has purchased you, and warriors to take you if he will not sell."

"My master paid eight thousand piasters for me, lost a ring worth twenty, and has kept me and been kind to me these many months. You will pay him the equivalent of thirty thousand, or more, if that will not suffice him."

Tserin drew a heavy purse from beneath his garments and looked at me inquiringly.

"I will not sell," I told him.

"What!" The captain scowled fiercely, and his hand sought his sword hilt.

"I have informed Lo Foo that I would not take her father's gold," I said. "She is free. If you must spend the money, give it to the poor who till the Prince's estates."

Tserin turned to Lo Foo. "I await Your Highness' commands," he said.

"It shall be as my master says," she told him. "I am free, and upon our return, the gold will be distributed to our poor. But this will be only on condition that I be permitted to assist him as I planned to do, before I go. And not until then will I consider myself free."

"But you must go at once," I said. "Your father needs you. Even a day's delay may mean that you will never see him again, alive."

"I am my father's daughter," she said, proudly, "and I know what he would have me do to uphold the honor of our house. Tserin, I will not require my slave-girls at present. Take your company outside the city and pitch the *yurts* where water and grass are plentiful. Then bring me two stout warriors. When I have done what I will do, then tomorrow or the next day, perhaps, we will start for home."

"Your lowly slave hastens to carry out Your Highness' commands," said the captain, making profound obeisance. Then he backed out the door.

* * * *

As soon as he had gone, Lo Foo called me to her side. "When you told me the story of your adventures with Mohammed Pasha, the despoiler," she said, "you mentioned a souterrain which connects this house with the one which Ahmed Aga has taken from you. I would like to know through which room in Ahmed's house one passes to enter this souterrain."

Hasan brought paper, pen and ink, and I quickly sketched for her a diagram of both houses, showing how the souterrain led from one to the other, and indicating, so that there could be no mistake, the room in Ahmed's *harim* through which the secret panel might be reached.

"Who knows of this secret passageway, other than you and Hasan Aga?" she asked.

"Musa the eunuch knows," I replied, "but I am sure he has told no one. Nor will he. He is loyal to the memory of Selma Hanoum, and to me."

"It is enough for my purpose if Ahmed Aga does not know," she said.

Then, taking with her the diagram I had made, she turned and went into the *harim*. When she came out she was cloaked and veiled as a *Moslemah*. To me, she said: "I think it best, my lord, that you go into the upper rooms and remain there for some time." To Hasan, she said: "It may be that Ahmed Aga will call on you, thinking you are my master, and offering to buy me from you. Make the price as high as he will pay, but sell me." Then she turned and went into the *salamlik*.

Hasan looked at me inquiringly.

"By Allah and again by Allah!" he exclaimed. "What is she up to now?"

"I know no more than you," I replied, "but you must trust and obey her." Then, leaving the old fellow muttering pious ejaculations in his beard, I mounted to the upper chambers and took my place at the latticed window.

9

After I had kept my vigil at the lattice for some time, I saw the opulent and perfidious Ahmed Aga riding toward home on his prancing, spirited steed, as was his custom at this hour of the day. Below me, I heard the door open, then saw Lo Foo step out into the street, a basket under her arm. As if she had not seen the *aga*, she walked straight in front of the spirited horse.

Ahmed reined up and roared: "*Wallah!* Look where you are going, *ya bint*!"

Lo Foo turned as if she had seen the *aga* for the first time, and with a swift motion drew aside her veil and shot him a languishing look from beneath the fringed curtains of her eyelids. Then she as swiftly replaced the veil, and turning, started off down the street.

Instantly the *aga* rode after her. But when she saw him coming, she turned as if frightened, and hurried back toward the house of Hasan.

Ahmed wheeled his prancing steed, rode after her once more, and dismounting, caught her by the arm. "Not so fast, my little *houri*," he said. "Be not afraid, but come with me to my house. I will cover you with pearls and diamonds, and you shall be the queen of my *harim*."

Lo Foo twisted her arm from his grasp. "Stop!" she exclaimed. "You know not what you are saying. I belong to Hasan Aga, and will enter no house save his."

"Perhaps Hasan Aga will sell you," suggested Ahmed, stroking his crisply curled beard and ogling her.

"Perhaps," she replied. "After all, another can cook and fetch and carry for him as well as I. He is an old man, and has no other use for me."

Ahmed eyed her hungrily. "But I am not an old man, little one, nor am I accounted unhandsome. And I'll swear I would find a more fitting occupation for such a budding flower than polishing pots and baking bread. What say you to a change of masters?"

Lo Foo lowered her gaze, coyly. "I must not forget that Hasan is still my master," she answered, softly.

"I'll go in and see him now," said Ahmed, starting for the door.

"Wait." She laid a restraining hand on his arm. "No use to go in now. He is not at home. Come tonight after the sunset prayer, and make no mention of our conversation, or he will be furious and refuse to sell me. Also, he will beat me, and it may be that he will kill me."

"Very well. I will come after the sunset prayer. And what is your name, that I may identify you?"

"I am his only slave-girl, so the name does not matter," she replied. "Merely tell him that your second wife saw me at the *hammam*, and would like to have me to serve her."

"I will be patient until after the sunset prayer," said Ahmed, swinging into his saddle. Lo Foo watched him ride away, then turned and entered the house.

* * * *

I hastened downstairs to meet her.

"You heard?" she asked.

"I both saw and heard," I replied. "Now what is to be done? Are we to capture him here in Hasan's house, when he calls to purchase you?"

"And bring suspicion on me and my house?" asked Hasan.

"Hardly," replied Lo Foo. "You, O uncle, will pretend that I am your slave-girl, when Ahmed comes to call on you this evening. You will agree to sell me, but only after extracting every last piaster you can from him. I will then go with him."

"Wait," I interposed. "I refuse to permit you to make such a sacrifice."

"But there will be no sacrifice, my lord," she said. "It is merely an adventure, and one which I shall enjoy."

"Ahmed *is* a handsome youth," I said, and could have bitten my tongue off the next instant when I saw her flush to the temples.

But her reply was calm enough. "You misunderstood, master. I fear no man, and am perfectly capable of taking care of myself. Now for the rest of the plan. As I have said, I will go with Ahmed Aga to his house. I will dance for him, and he will desire me. But I will refuse to go with him into any room, save the one which has the secret panel that connects with the souterrain. That is why I asked you for a diagram of the house. I had to know that room beyond any shadow of doubt. You, my master, will be waiting behind the panel. Tserin will be with you, and two of his warriors will stand at the bottom of the ladder to assist in case of trouble.

But you must not, under any consideration, enter the room until I sign for you to do so, no matter what takes place."

"There is too much danger to you in this plan," I said. "I refuse to be a party to it. I prefer to leave Ahmed to his ill-gotten gains, rather than put you in such peril."

"Then, for this once, my lord, I must disobey you. Either you will carry out my plan as I have outlined it, or I will enter the house of the *aga* myself, at the first opportunity."

Whereupon, there being nothing else left for me to do, I agreed.

Shortly thereafter, Tserin returned with two warriors. All three made obeisance before Lo Foo, and she set the warriors to preparing our evening meal. After we had eaten, the three Mongols declined *narghiles*, but smoked, instead, their strange, baton-like pipes with tiny brass bowls, each of which held only a pinch of tobacco.

Presently there was a knock at the front door, and all of us except Hasan scurried hastily back into the next room. We heard him admit the young *aga*. Then he clapped his hands, and Lo Foo went out to serve pipes and coffee.

For more than an hour we sat there, smoking and waiting, while Hasan dickered with his guest. Then Lo Foo came in and hastily gathered some of her belongings into a bundle. "The poisoner bought me for thirty-five thousand piasters," she said. "I am going with him now. Don't fail to be behind the panel at the end of the souterrain, as planned."

"We will be there," I assured her.

Then she was gone.

10

An hour later, I stood at the top of the ladder in the end of the souterrain, peering through the peephole in the panel. I was looking into an empty bedchamber in the *harim* of Ahmed Aga, the chamber which had once been Selma Hanoum's and mine.

There drifted to me, from the *majlis*, the throbbing of drums and the shrilling of hautboys; so I knew there was dancing—that presently Lo Foo would dance before the *aga*, and if all went well, would enter that very room with him.

And so it came to pass. For presently the music ceased, and I heard voices in the hallway outside the door—the voices of Ahmed Aga and Lo Foo. The *aga* was saying: "This house is yours, my little dove. Choose from among all the rooms which one you will, and if it is occupied the occupant must vacate in your favor. But choose quickly, light of my eyes, for you have so fired me with desire that I am consumed with waiting."

They stopped before the door, and I heard Lo Foo say: "I like this room, my lord."

"It is the room of Salamah, my first wife," said Ahmed, "but she is fortunately visiting her mother. This room it shall be. Ho, Musa, guard this door, and see that we are not disturbed."

I heard the familiar tones of Musa, as he replied: "Harkening and obedience, *sidi*." Then Lo Foo entered, carrying a small bundle of her belongings. She was followed by Ahmed, who closed and bolted the door.

As I have said, Lo Foo had danced before me many times, but always in the silken raiment of her native land. Never before had I seen her in the abbreviated costume of a gipsy dancing-girl, and I was lost in wonder and admiration at the beauty it revealed. Glittering shields of beaded openwork covered breasts so perfect that to ornament them was like painting the lily. About her slender waist was clasped a jeweled girdle, from which depended a skirt of filmy black material through which the white gleam of her shapely limbs was plainly visible. Except for the customary bracelets, anklets and rings, she wore no other clothing or ornaments.

Perfectly imitating the sinuous gait of a gipsy dancing-girl, she walked to the *diwan* and stretched her slim, alluring form upon it.

His face aflame with passion, Ahmed began tearing off his clothes and flinging them right and left as if he would never want them again. When he had stripped to his soft, silken shirt and skull-cap, he hurled himself at the princess like a tiger springing upon its prey.

At this juncture, I could scarcely restrain myself from opening the panel and leaping into the room, simitar in hand. But because of the positive injunctions Lo Foo had put upon me, I refrained.

A moment later I saw why she had so instructed me—and marveled. As Ahmed came toward her, she rose to meet him, and grasping his wrist with both hands, turned and drew it across her shoulder. A downward pull on the arm, and a slight heave of her shapely back, assisted by the amorous *aga's* own momentum, sent him catapulting through the air. Feet up and head down, he struck the wall with his back, an impact that must have knocked the breath from his body. Then he fell in a crumpled heap upon the *diwan*.

Lo Foo quickly bent over him and struck him a sharp blow behind the ear with the edge of her hand. Then she signed to me.

I opened the panel and stepped into the room, followed by Tserin.

From outside the door came the voice of Musa. "What was that noise, *sidi*? Shall I break in?"

"Answer him," whispered Lo Foo. "Say everything is all right."

"We were playing at tag and overturned a chest, Musa," I called, imitating the voice of Ahmed. "Pay no attention, and keep good watch."

"I hear and obey, *sidi*," was the reply.

"Now, my lord," Lo Foo whispered, "you must quickly exchange clothing with this poisoner, for he may recover consciousness soon. Tserin will help you."

With the aid of the Mongol captain, I swiftly removed my clothing and donned the silken shirt and skull-cap of Ahmed. While we were dressing him in my garments, Lo Foo opened her bundle and busied herself laying out cosmetics and heating a small curling-iron in a candle flame.

When all was in readiness, she trimmed and curled my black beard, and then, looking from Ahmed's features to my own, applied deft touches here and there from her tray. Presently she held up a mirror before me, and I started back in amazement at the image I saw therein, for it was the face of Ahmed Aga.

Lo Foo turned to Tserin. "Take this carrion to the house of Hasan," she said, indicating the senseless form of Ahmed. "Shave off his beard, bind him hand and foot, and see that he does not escape."

The captain went to the open panel and softly called his two warriors. They came to the top of the ladder, and we passed the limp form of the *aga* to them.

"You may go now, Tserin," said Lo Foo. "Tell Hasan Aga that tomorrow my master will call upon him by way of the front door, and I by way of the souterrain."

He bowed low, and followed his men down the ladder.

* * * *

Lo Foo closed the panel. "We must sleep now, my lord," she said. "Tomorrow will be a trying day, for with my help you must establish yourself as Ahmed Aga in this household."

"There is but one *diwan*," I said. "I will sleep on the floor, and you may have it."

"Why, it is a large *diwan*, and there is ample room for both," she said. "Yet if you object to sleeping with me, it is I who will lie on the floor."

"It is not that I object to sleeping with you," I replied, "but that I believed you would object to sleeping with me."

"Not at all," she assured me. "Why should I?"

"Why, er, it's not customary," I stammered.

"For a slave-girl to sleep with her master? Why, it is common practise, both in your land and mine, and has been throughout the ages. You yourself told me how the great and holy Daoud, slayer of the giant Goliath, and father of Suleiman the Wise, slept with a virgin when very old, to gain warmth for his aged bones."

Her argument was unanswerable, yet I knew that if I occupied the diwan with her, I should be expected to sleep. And I was certain that if Malik Daoud himself, in the years of his utmost senility, had this ravishing little beauty beside him instead of Abishag the Shunammite virgin, he would not have slept a wink, either.

"I am not sleepy," I told her. "Do you get some sleep, and I will sit and smoke."

"No, my lord. If you can not sleep, then you must rest, at least." Gently she pushed me back upon the *diwan*. Seeing that there was no escape, I stretched out, turned my face to the wall, and closed my eyes.

With tender solicitude she threw a coverlet over me. Then I heard her removing her jewelry and bangles and placing them on a taboret. A moment later the *diwan* gave almost imperceptibly under the slight pressure of her body, and I sensed the gentle warmth and intoxicating fragrance of her, there beside me.

By the sound of her faint, regular breathing, I knew that Lo Foo soon slept. But I could not. Although it had been my intention to remain all night with my face to the wall, I soon found this a most uncomfortable arrangement. As says the old proverb: "All are not asleep whose eyes are closed," so it was with me. And though I counted sheep, goats and camels in my mind's eye, until I had numbered more of these animals than are to be found in all Arabia, I only grew the wider awake, and so fidgety that I could scarce restrain myself from leaping up and shouting.

Presently, when it seemed that my entire left side was dead, and that millions of tiny, tantalizing imps were fingering all my nerve ends, I found that I must turn on my back. This I contrived to do very quietly, and without touching her who slept beside me, blissfully unconscious of the agony I was undergoing.

What a relief! With a pricking like that of a thousand needles, circulation was restored to my left side, and the imps ceased to pluck at my nerves. Now, as I lay there in a little more comfort, I decided to give over counting sheep, and as sleep was impossible, think of the important things I must do on the morrow.

But sleep, it seems, is a fickle mistress. No sooner did I cease to court her, and begin conning my plans for the coming day, than a drowsiness assailed me, and I passed into dreamland.

My dream carried me back to the old happy days when Selma Hanoum and I slept, side by side, on this very *diwan*. I must have turned on my right side shortly thereafter, for the dream ended, and I awoke to that elusive sense of reality which comes in a half-sleeping, half-waking state. Perhaps I had thrown my arm across Lo Foo in my sleep, for it appeared to be a tactile sensation, the velvety feel of her, that had caused my dream to vanish. Yet, some-how, I was not sure but that this was another dream. Dimly, I recall that a soft hand took mine, removed it just a little from the position it had occupied, and held it. Then once more slumber claimed me.

11

Bright sunlight streaming down upon my face, awakened me. For a moment, I did not realize where I was. Then I recognized the familiar decorations and furnishings of the room that had been mine and Selma Hanoum's for many happy months.

Lo Foo had donned her native silken garments, and was comb-ing her glossy black hair. But when she saw that I was awake, she sprang up and unbolted the door.

A slave-girl entered with a ewer of water and a basin. I made ablution and prayed the dawn prayer, after which another slave-girl brought coffee and breakfast.

When she had gone out, Lo Foo bolted the door once more. "While you slept, I had breakfast," she said, "and then went about, meeting the inmates of this house. Today, I think it best that you do not ride forth, as is Ahmed Aga's custom, to attend the Pasha, but send a slave to him, pleading illness. Many of the inmates you will know, as the *aga* kept most of Selma Hanoum's slaves. But when you see one you do not recognize, stroke your beard three times in succession, and I will call that person by name, so you will make no mistakes."

After breakfast, I went forth into the *majlis*, and Lo Foo kept constantly at my side. "Remember," she whispered, "Hamed the Dragoman is no more. You are Ahmed Aga. Cultivate his manner-isms, speak as he would speak, and in private, copy his signature until you can duplicate it perfectly without the slightest hesita-tion."

Things came about as Lo Foo had predicted, while I marveled at her foresight, and though I feared that at least one of the slaves who had served me for many months would recognize me, none did so. Before midday I knew the name of every inmate of the house who had been a stranger to me.

Ahmed, I learned, had two wives, but fortunately, no children. The second, I triple-divorced that morning, paying her double her dowry and sending her back to her parents. The other, who was visiting her mother, I resolved to divorce upon her return. His hostlers, slave-girls and eunuchs, most of whom had been Selma's, I retained for the present.

That afternoon I ordered Ahmed's prancing charger brought out, and rode to the house of Hasan, resolved to deal with Ahmed himself. I would give him a simitar with which to defend himself, and felt confident that the will of Allah would prevail for the right.

Lo Foo, meanwhile, was to lock herself in the bedroom, then pass through the souterrain into Hasan's house.

* * * *

I was about to dismount before my old friend's door, when I noticed a hooting, jeering rabble coming down the street, following four men who bore a much bedraggled body on a crude stretcher. This sight aroused my curiosity, and I remained in my saddle to watch them pass.

As they drew closer, I saw, with a start of surprize, that the corpse wore the same clothing I had worn the day before, and greatly resembled me as I looked before I had grown a beard. The clothing was sodden, and water dripped from it into the dust of the street.

"Has some one been drowned?" I asked a camel-driver, who trailed along at the edge of the crowd.

"A vile malefactor has reaped his just reward," he replied. "The corpse of that foul murderer and wife-poisoner, Hamed the Dragoman, who escaped the executioner some months ago, was seen floating in the Tigris, and some fishermen just hauled it out."

Swiftly I dismounted, and gave my reins to a groom, who had followed me on foot. Hasan answered my knock, and led me into the *majlis*. Tserin and his two warriors were there, smoking their baton-like pipes, but Lo Foo had not yet arrived.

"Where is Ahmed Aga?" I asked.

Hasan looked at me slyly, and winked at Tserin. "Why, you are Ahmed Aga," he replied.

"If I am Ahmed Aga, then where is Hamed the Dragoman?"

At this moment, Lo Foo entered, and the three Mongols instantly bowed to the floor before her.

"What have you done with the prisoner?" she demanded. "Why isn't one of you guarding him?"

Hasan cleared his throat. "The base and inhuman monster has met with the justice of Allah," he said. "Last night when he was brought in, I recalled that he was the poisoner of my sister's daughter, on whom be peace, and that his blood-wreak belonged to me. I would have slit his throat, but Tserin had noticed a thriving young bamboo sprout in my garden. He reminded me that, through the machinations of this villain, my nephew came near to meeting death by impalement, and explained how, in Cathay, they have a singularly effective way of letting nature perform such tasks. The dog died before daybreak this morning, and we flung him into the Tigris, after putting papers on his person which would positively identify him as Hamed the Dragoman."

"I can not find the heart to be angry with you, uncle," I said, "though you have stolen the vengeance which belonged to me."

"*Waha!*" he replied. "We but made a bride of him, instead of a groom. He would have been groom to a tiger lily, but instead, we made him bride of a bamboo."

The three Mongols, it seemed, were not to get off so easily. Lo Foo spoke rapidly to them in their own tongue. It was apparent that she was furiously angry and they were very much frightened.

"Forgive them, Lo Foo," I said. "After all, the affair was more Hasan's doings than theirs."

So she relented, and after a pipe and a cup of coffee with Hasan, we returned to the palace, I on my horse, and she by way of the souterrain.

12

That night I sat in the *majlis* of my *harim*, an opulent *aga* with wealth, land and slaves, and the finest home in Mosul. Wearing rich silks and costly jewels, and reclining amid the soft cushions of my luxurious *diwan*, I was surrounded by slave-girls, eager to court my favor and do my bidding.

Behind a screen at the far end of the *majlis*, musicians were tuning their instruments. And in one of the rear rooms, Lo Foo, with the assistance of two of my slave-girls, was spending much time over her toilette. She was to dance before me that night, her dance of farewell, for on the morrow she would leave Mosul for ever.

Presently I heard the tinkle of anklets in the hallway, and Lo Foo entered. Musa, the eunuch, signed to the musicians behind the screen, and they began to play.

Then Lo Foo danced.

Never before had I seen her so beautiful, so radiant, or so madly alluring. The key color of the ensemble she had chosen for that dance was red, the color of love. Her skirt was a tenuous, diaphanous material of a shade that matched the red of her lips, and was suspended on a girdle of cloth of gold, studded with rubies. Her breast shields were blood-red coral beads, woven on golden threads, and her anklets and armlets were gold, decked with figures of red lacquer.

The dance was one of passionate love—of wooing and of mating. Never had she danced thus before me, and never had I been so powerfully affected. The throbbing music, the rhythmic swaying of her slim, young body, and the matchless perfection of her face and figure, held me enthralled. Forgotten were my sorrow and my affliction, which had, up to this time, hung before my eyes as a veil, blinding me to the true worth of her who danced before me, to the fact that I loved Lo Foo—had loved her since first I saw her there in the slave mart.

Suddenly I realized that the dance was over. The music had ceased, and the little dancer had flung herself down before me. I caught her up, and she nestled in my arms like a tired child. But her eyes were the eyes of a woman, and they were starry with a light which a man, though he see it but once, may never mistake. The fragrance of her breath intoxicated me like heady wine. Unmindful of the slave-girls and the eunuch, I claimed the sweetness of her lips. Her arms stole about my neck, and clung. Still holding her in my arms, I stood up, and carrying her into our room, gently lowered her to the *diwan*.

Behind me, Musa, the eunuch, closed the door.

Gently I unclasped the soft arms from around my neck.

"I can not remain here with you tonight, Lo Foo," I said. "I will go through the souterrain to the house of Hasan."

"But why?"

"Because I love you."

She clung to me, would not let me go, and again those starry lights in her eyes thrilled me.

"Stay, my lord," she pleaded. "I have always loved you. And now I love you so much that it hurts."

* * * *

As on the morning previous, I was awakened by the sun shining in my face. Lo Foo, I thought, had gone out into the *harim* for her breakfast. For some time I lay there, indolently blinking in the sunlight, reviewing glorious memories.

But presently, as Lo Foo did not put in an appearance, I sat up. Then I saw a note lying on the taboret beside the *diwan*, and recognized the painfully scrawled handwriting of my little princess, who, despite my patient teaching, wrote wretched Arabic. My heart fell as I read the note. It said:

> Beloved:
>
> It would have been easier for me to pluck my heart, bleeding and quivering from my bosom, than to leave you thus. But a daughter's first duty is to her parents, and my dying father needs me. I can not remain to say farewell, for in your arms my will deserts me. So this is the only way.
>
> Farewell, and may the God of your people and the Gods of my ancestors watch over you. I will always love you.
>
> Your broken-hearted,
>
> Lo Foo.

I dressed hastily, and dashing out into the *majlis*, called for my horse. A few moments later, I was riding madly through the streets of Mosul. Presently I passed the city gate, and came to the place where the Mongols had camped. The circular places showed where the *yurts* had stood, but not a single peg remained.

For a time I entertained the insane idea of following Lo Foo's caravan. But reason told me that I could never hope to overtake the swift Mongol riders. And even if this were accomplished, it would only increase the agony of our parting.

Accordingly, I turned my horse, and sadly rode back to my desolate house.

* * * *

Two years passed, during which I sought forgetfulness by giving myself up to the pleasures which my great wealth commanded for me. Then, one day, a Mongol called at my house. He had come through with a caravan of traders from Cathay. After handing me a small parcel, he made obeisance and withdrew.

With trembling hands I undid the parcel. It contained a small, richly fashioned jade locket, and a folded bit of parchment. I sprang the catch of the locket, and there smiled out at me the features of a handsome baby boy, done in life-like colors. Unfolding the parchment, I read: "Thy son, and mine, beloved." There was no signature, but a royal seal held by its stem a dried and lacquered tiger lily.

And thus, *effendi*, there passed out of my life the rare and beautiful flower from far Cathay. But, though she was not a *Moslemah*, I have never ceased to love her—may Allah forgive me!—nor will I, so long as there is life within me.

Ho, Silat! Bring the sweet and take the full.

THE THING OF A
THOUSAND SHAPES

CHAPTER 1

Uncle Jim was dead. I could scarcely believe it, but the little yellow missive, which had just been handed to me by the Western Union messenger boy, left no room for doubt. It was short and convincing:

> Come to Peoria at once. James Braddock dead of heart failure.
> Corbin & His Attorneys.

I should explain here that Uncle Jim, my mother's brother, was my only living near relative. Having lost both father and mother in the Iroquois Theatre Fire at the age of twelve years, I should have been forced to abandon my plans for a high school and commercial education but for his noble generosity. In his home town he was believed to be comfortably well off, but I had learned not long since that it had meant a considerable sacrifice for him to furnish the fifteen hundred dollars a year to put me through high school and business college, and I was glad when the time came for me to find employment, and thus become independent of his bounty. My position as bookkeeper for a commission firm in South Water Street, while not particularly remunerative, at least provided a comfortable living, and I was happy in it—until the message of his death came.

I took the telegram to my employer, obtained a week's leave-of-absence, and was soon on the way to the Union Depot.

All the way to Peoria I thought about Uncle Jim. He was not old—only forty-five—and when I had last seen him he had seemed particularly hale and hearty. This sudden loss of my nearest and dearest friend was, therefore, almost unbelievable. I carried a leaden weight in my heart, and it seemed that the lump in my throat would choke me.

Uncle Jim had lived on a three-hundred-and-twenty acre farm near Peoria. Being a bachelor, he had employed a housekeeper. The farm work was looked after by a family named Severs—man, wife and two sons—who lived in the tenant house, perhaps a thousand feet to the rear of the owner's residence, in convenient proximity to the barn, silos and other farm buildings.

As I have said, my uncle's neighbors believed him to be comfortably well off, but I knew the place was mortgaged to the limit, so that the income from the fertile acres was practically absorbed by overhead expenses and interest.

Had my uncle been a business man in the true sense of the term, no doubt he could have been wealthy. But he was a scientist and dreamer, inclined to let the farm run itself while he devoted his time to study and research. His hobby was psychic phenomena. His thirst for more facts regarding the human mind was insatiable. In the pursuit of his favorite study, he had attended seances in this country and abroad with the leading spiritualists of the world.

He was a member of the London Society for Psychical Research, as well as the American Society, and corresponded regularly with noted scientists, psychologists and spiritualists. As an authority on psychic phenomena, he had contributed articles to the leading scientific publications from time to time, and was the author of a dozen well-known books on the subject.

Thus, grief-filled though I was, my mind kept presenting to me memory after memory of Uncle Jim's scientific attainments and scholarly life, while the rumbling car wheels left the miles behind; and the thought that such a man had been lost to me and to the world was almost unbearable.

I arrived in Peoria shortly before midnight, and was glad to find Joe Severs, son of my uncle's tenant, waiting for me with a flivver. After a five-mile ride in inky darkness over a rough road, we came to the farm.

I was greeted at the door by the housekeeper, Mrs. Rhodes, and one of two men, nearby neighbors, who had kindly volunteered to "set up" with the corpse. The woman's eyes were red with weeping, and her tears flowed afresh as she led me to the room where my uncle's body lay in a gray casket.

A dim kerosene lamp burned in one comer of the room, and after the silent watcher had greeted me with a handclasp and a sad shake of the head, I walked up to view the remains of my dearest friend on earth.

As I looked down on that noble, kindly face, the old lump, which had for a time subsided, came back in my throat. I expected tears, heartrending sobs, but they did not come. I seemed dazed— bewildered.

Suddenly, and apparently against my own reason, I heard myself saying aloud, "He is not dead—only sleeping."

When the watchers looked at me in amazement I repeated, "Uncle Jim is *not dead*! He is only sleeping."

Mrs. Rhodes looked compassionately at me, and by a meaning glance at the others said as plainly as if she had spoken, "His mind is affected."

She and Mr. Newberry, the neighbor whom I had first met, gently led me from the room. I was, myself dumfounded at the words I had uttered, nor could I find a reason for them.

My uncle was undoubtedly dead, at least as far as this physical world was concerned. There was nothing about the appearance of the pale, rigid corpse to indicate life, and he had, without doubt, been pronounced dead by a physician. Why. then, had I made this unusual, uncalled for—in fact, ridiculous—statement? I did not know, I concluded that I must have been crazed with grief — beside myself for the moment.

I had announced my intention to keep watch with Mr. Newberry and the other neighbor, Mr. Glitch, but was finally prevailed upon to go to my room, on the ground that my nerves were overwrought and I must have rest. It was decided, therefore, that the housekeeper, who had scarcely slept a wink the night before, and I should retire, while the two neighbors alternately kept two hour watches, one sitting up while the other slept on a davenport near the fireplace.

Mrs. Rhodes conducted me to my room. I quickly undressed, blew out the kerosene light and got into bed. It was some time before I could compose myself for sleep, and I remember that just as I was dozing off I seemed to hear my name pronounced as if someone were calling me from a great distance:

"Billy!" and then, in the same far-away voice: *"Save me, Billy!"*

I had slept for perhaps fifteen minutes when I awoke with a start. Either I was dreaming, or something about the size and shape of a half-grown conger eel was creeping across my bed.

For the moment I was frozen with horror, as I perceived the white, nameless thing, in the dim light from my window. With a convulsive movement I threw the bedclothes from me, leaped to the floor, struck a match, and quickly lit the lamp. Then, taking my heavy walking-stick in hand, I advanced on the bed.

Moving the bedclothing cautiously with the stick and prodding here and there, I at length discovered that the thing was gone. The door was closed, there was no transom, and the window was screened. I therefore concluded that it must still be in the room.

With this thought in mind, I carefully searched every inch of space, looking under and behind the furniture, with the lamp in one hand and stick in the other. I then removed all the bedding and opened the dresser drawers, and found—nothing!

After completely satisfying myself that the animal I had seen, or perhaps seemed to see, could not possibly be in the room I decided that I had been suffering from a nightmare, and again retired. Because of my nervousness from the experience, I did not again blow out the light, but instead turned it low.

After a half hour of restless turning and tossing, I succeeded in going to sleep; this time for possibly twenty minutes, when I was once more aroused. The same feeling of horror came over me, as I distinctly heard a rolling, scraping sound beneath my bed. I kept perfectly still and waited while the sound went on. Something was apparently creeping underneath my bed, and it seemed to be moving toward the foot, slowly and laboriously.

Stealthily I sat up, leaned forward and peered over the footboard. The sounds grew more distinct, and a white, round mass, which looked like a porcupine rolled into a ball with bristles projecting, emerged from under my bed. I uttered a choking cry of fright, and the thing *disappeared before my eyes!*

Without waiting to search the room further, I leaped from the bed to the spot nearest the door, wrenched it open, and started on a run for the living-room, attired only in pajamas. As I neared the room, however, part of my lost courage came back to me, and I slowed down to a walk. I reasoned that precipitate entrance into the room would arouse the household, and that possibly, after all, I was only the victim of a second nightmare. I resolved, therefore, to say nothing to the watchers about my experience, but to tell them only that I was unable to sleep and had come down for company.

Newberry met me at the door.

"Why what's the matter?" he asked, "You look pale. Anything wrong?"

"Nothing but a slight attack of indigestion. Couldn't sleep, so I came down for company."

"You should have brought a dressing-gown or something. You may take cold."

"Oh I feel quite comfortable enough." I said. Newberry stirred the logs in the fireplace to a blaze, and we moved our chairs close to the flickering circle of warmth. The dim light was still burning in the corner of the room, and Glitch was snoring on the davenport.

"Funny thing," said Newberry, "the instructions your uncle left."

"Instructions? What instructions?" I asked.

"Why, didn't you know? But of course you didn't. He left written instructions with Mrs. Rhodes that in case of his sudden death his body was not to be embalmed, packed in ice, or preserved in any way, and that it was not to be buried under any consideration, until decomposition had set in. He also ordered that no autopsy should be held until it had been definitely decided that putrefaction had taken place."

"Have these instructions been carried out?" I asked.

"To the letter," he replied.

"And how long will it take for putrefaction to set in?"

"The doctors say it will probably be noticed in twenty-four hours."

I reflected on this strange order of my uncle's. It seemed to me that he must have feared being buried alive, or something of the sort, and I recalled several instances, of which I had heard, where bodies, upon being exhumed, were found turned over in their coffins, while others had apparently torn their hair and clawed the lid in their efforts to escape from a living tomb.

I was beginning to feel sleepy again and had just started to doze, when Newberry grasped my arm.

"Look!" he exclaimed, pointing toward the body.

I looked quickly and seemed to see something white for an instant, near the nostrils.

"Did you see it?" he asked breathlessly.

"See what?" I replied, wishing to learn if he had seen the same thing I had.

"I saw something white, like a thick vapor or filmy veil, come out of his nose. When I spoke to you it seemed to jerk back. Didn't you see it?"

"Thought I saw a white flash there when you spoke, but it must have been imagination."

The time had now arrived for Glitch to watch, so my companion awakened him, and they exchanged places. Newberry was soon asleep, and Glitch, being a stoical German, said little. I presently became drowsy, and was asleep in my chair in a short time.

A cry from Glitch brought me to my feet. "Vake up and help catch der cat!"

"What cat?" demanded Newberry, also awakening.

"Der big vite cat," said Glitch, visibly excited. "Chust now he came der door through and yumped der coffin in."

The three of us rushed to the coffin, but there was no sign of a cat, and everything seemed undisturbed.

"Dot's funny," said Glitch. "Maybe it's hiding someveres in der room."

We searched the room, without result.

"You've been seeing things," said Newberry.

"What did the animal look like?" I asked.

"Vite, und big as a dog. It kommt der door in, so, und gallped across der floor, so, und yumped in der casket chust like dot. *Ach!* It vos a fierce-looking beast."

Glitch was very much in earnest and gesticulated rapidly as he described the appearance and movements of the feline. Perhaps I should have felt inclined to laugh, had it not been for my own experience that night. I noticed, too, that Newberry's expression was anything but jocular.

It was now nearly four o'clock, time for Newberry to watch, but Glitch protested that he could not sleep another wink, so the three of us drew chairs up close to the fire. On each side of the fireplace was a large window. The shades were completely drawn and the windows were draped with heavy lace curtains. Happening to look up at the window to the left, I noticed something of a mouse-gray color hanging near the top of one of the curtains. As I looked, I fancied I saw a slight movement as of a wing being stretched a bit and then folded, and the thing took on the appearance of a large vampire bat, hanging upside down.

I called the attention of my companions to our singular visitor, and both saw it as plainly as I.

"How do you suppose he got in?" asked Newberry.

"Funny ve didn't see him before," said Glitch.

I picked up the fire tongs and Newberry seized the poker. Creeping softly up to the curtain, I stood on tiptoe and reached up to seize the animal with the tongs. It was too quick for me, However, and fluttered out of my reach. There followed a chase around the room. Which lasted several minutes. Seeing that it would be impossible for us to capture the creature by this method, we gave up the chase, whereupon it calmed down and suspended itself from the picture molding, upside down.

On seeing this, Glitch, who had taken a heavy book from the table, hurled it at our unwelcome visitor. His aim was good, and the thing uttered a *squeak* as it was crushed against the wall.

At this moment I thought I heard a moan from the direction of the casket, but could not be certain.

Newberry and I rushed over to where the book had fallen, intent on dispatching the thing with poker and thongs, but only the book lay on the floor. The creature had *completely disappeared.*

I picked up the book, and noticed, as I did so, a grayish smear on the back cover. Taking this over to the light, we saw that it had a soapy appearance. As we looked the substance apparently became absorbed. Either by the atmosphere or into the cloth cover of the book. There remained, however, a dry, white, faintly-defined splotch on the book cover.

"What do you make of it?" I asked them.

"Strange!" said Newberry.

I turned to Glitch, and noticed for the first time that his eyes were wide with fear. He shook his head and cast furtive glaces toward the casket.

"What do *you* think it is?" I asked.

"A vampire, maybe. A *real* vampire."

"What do you mean by a real vampire?"

Glitch then described how, in the folk lore of his native land, there were stories current of corpses which lived on in the grave. It was believed that the spirits of these corpses assumed the form of huge vampire bats at night, and went about sucking the blood of living persons, with which they would return to the grave from time to time and nourish the corpse. This proceeding was kept up indefinitely, unless the corpse were exhumed and a stake driven through the heart.

He related, in particular, the story of a Hungarian named Arnold Paul, whose body was dug up after it had been buried forty days. It was found that his cheeks were flushed with blood, and that his hair, beard and nails had grown in the grave. When the stake was driven through his heart, he had uttered a frightful shriek and a torrent of blood gushed from his mouth.

The vampire story seized on my imagination in a peculiar way. I thought again of my uncle's strange request regarding the disposition of his body, and of the strange apparitions I had seen. For the moment I was a convert to the vampire theory.

My better judgment, however, soon convinced me that there could not be such a thing as a vampire, and, even if there were, a man whose character had been so noble as that of my deceased uncle would most certainly never resort to such hideous and revolting practices.

We sat together in silence as the first faint streaks of dawn showed in the east. A few minutes later the welcome aroma of coffee and frying bacon greeted our nostrils, and Mrs. Rhodes came into announce that breakfast was ready.

After breakfast, my newly-made friends departed for their homes, both assuring me that they would be glad to come and watch with me again that night.

However, I read something in the uneasy manner of Glitch which led me to believe that I could not count on him, and I was, therefore, not greatly surprised when he telephone me an hour later, stating that his wife was ill, and that he would not be able to come.

CHAPTER 2

I strolled outdoors to enjoy a cigar, comforted by the rays of the morning sun after my night's experience.

It was pleasant, I reflected, to be once more in the realm of the natural, to see the trees attired in the autumn foliage, to feel the rustle of fallen leaves underfoot, to fill my lungs with the spicy, invigorating October air.

A gray squirrel scampered across my pathway, his cheek pouches bulging with acorns. A flock of blackbirds, migrating southward, stopped for a few moments in the trees above my head, chattering vociferously; then resumed their journey with a sudden *whirr* of wings and a few hoarse notes of farewell.

"It is but a step," I reflected, "from the natural to the supernatural."

This observation started a new line of thought. After all, could anything be supernatural—above nature? Nature, according to my belief, was only another name for God, eternal mind, omnipotent, omnipresent, omniscient ruler of the universe. If He were omnipotent, could anything take place contrary to His laws? Obviously not.

The word "supernatural" was, after all, only an expression invented by man in his finite ignorance, to define those things which he did not understand. Telegraphy, telephony, the phonograph, the moving picture—all would have been regarded with superstition by an age less advanced than ours. Man had only to become familiar with the laws governing them, in order to discard the word "supernatural" as applied to their manifestations.

What right, then, had I to term the phenomena, which I had just witnessed, supernatural? I might call them supernormal, but to think of them as supernatural would be to believe the impossible: namely, that that which is all-powerful had been overpowered.

I resolved, then and there, that if further phenomena manifest-
ed themselves that night, I would, as far as it were possible, curb
my superstition and fear, regard them with the eye of a philoso-
pher, and endeavor to learn their cause, which must necessarily be
governed by natural law.

A gray cloud of dust and the whirring of a motor announced
the coming of an automobile. The next minute an ancient flivver, with whose bumps of eccentricity I had gained some acquain-
tance, turned into the driveway and stopped opposite me. Joe Severs, older son of my uncle's tenant, stepped out and came running
toward me.

"Glitch's wife died this morning," he panted, "and he swears
Mr. Braddock is a vampire and sucked her blood."

"What rot!" I replied. "Nobody believes him, of course?"

"I ain't so sure of that," said Joe. "Some of the farmers are
takin' it mighty serious. One of the Langdon boys, first farm north
of here, was took sick this mornin'. Doctor don't know what's the
matter of him. Folks say it looks mighty queer."

Mrs. Rhodes appeared on the front porch.

"A telephone call for you, sir," she said.

I hastened to the phone. A woman was speaking.

"This is Mrs. Newberry," she said. "My husband is dreadfully
ill, and asked me to tell you that he cannot come to sit up with you
tonight."

I thanked the lady, offered my condolences, and tendered my
sincere wishes for her husband's speedy recovery. This done, I
wrote a note of sympathy to Mr. Glitch, and dispatched Joe with it.

Here, indeed, was a pretty situation. Glitch's wife dead, Newberry seriously ill, and the whole countryside, frightened by this
impossible vampire story! I knew it would be useless to ask any
of the other neighbors to keep watch with me. Obviously, I was
destined to face the terrors of the coming night alone. Was I equal
to the task? Could my nerves, already unstrung by the previous
night's experience, withstand the ordeal?

I must confess, and not without a feeling of shame, that at this
juncture I felt impelled to flee, anywhere, and leave my deceased
uncle's affairs to shape themselves as they would.

With this idea in mind, I repaired to my room and started to pack my grip. Something fell to the floor. It was my uncle's last letter, received only the day before the telegram arrived announcing his death. I hesitated—then picked it up and opened it. The last paragraph help my attention:

> And, Billy, my boy, don't worry any more about the money I advanced you. It was, as you say, a considerable drain my resources, but I gave it willingly, gladly, for the education of my sister's son. My only regret is that I could not have done more.
> Affectionately,
>
> Uncle Jim.

A flush of guilt came over me. The reproach of my conscience was keen and painful. I had been about to commit a cowardly, dishonorable deed.

"Thank God, for the accidental intervention of that letter." I said fervently.

My resolution was firmly made now, I would see the thing through at all costs. The noble love, the generous self-sacrifice of my uncle, should not go unrequited.

I quickly unpacked my bag and walked downstairs. The rest of the day was uneventful, but the night—how I dreaded the coming of the night! As I stood on the porch and watched the last faint glow of the sunset slowly fading, I wished that I, liked Joshua, might cause the sun and moon to stand still.

Twilight came on all too quickly, accelerated by a bank of heavy clouds which appeared on the western horizon: and darkness succeeded twilight with unwanted rapidity.

I entered the house and trod the hallway leading to the living-room, with much the same feeling, no doubt, that a convict experiences when entering the death cell.

The housekeeper was just placing the lamp, freshly cleaned and filled, in the room. Joe Severs' younger brother, Sam, had placed logs in the fireplace, with kindling and paper beneath them, ready for lighting. Mrs. Rhodes bade me a kindly "Good-night, sir," and departed noiselessly.

At last the dreaded moment had arrived. I was alone with the nameless powers of darkness.

I shuddered involuntarily. A damp chill pervaded the air, and I ignited the kindling beneath the logs in the fireplace. Then, drawing the shades to shut out the pitch blackness of the night, I lighted my pipe and stood in the warm glow.

Under the genial influence of pipe and warmth, my feeling of fear was temporarily dissipated. Taking a book from the library table, I settled down to read. It was called "The Reality of Materialization Phenomena," and had been written by my uncle. The publishers were Bulwer & Sons, New York and London.

It was apparently a record of the observations made by my uncle at materialization seances in this country and Europe. Contrary to my usual custom on starting a book, I read the author's introduction. He began by expressing the wish that those who might read the work should first lay aside all prejudice and all preconceived ideas regarding the subject, which were not based on positive knowledge: then weigh the facts as he had found them before drawing a definite conclusion.

The following passage, in particular, held my attention:

> While it is to be admitted, with regret, that there are many people calling themselves mediums, who deceive their sitters nightly and whose productions are consequently mere optical illusions, produced my chicanery and legerdemain, the writer has nevertheless gathered, at the sittings recorded in this book, where all possibility of fraud was excluded by rigorous examination and control, undeniable evidence that genuine materialization are, and can be, produced.
>
> The source and physical composition—if indeed it be physical—of a phantasm materialized by a true medium, remains up to the present time, inexplicable. That such manifestations are not a hallucinations, has been proved time and again by taking photographs One would indeed be compelled to strain his credulity to the utmost, were he to believe that a mere hallucination could be photographed.
>
> As I have stated, the exact nature and source of the phenomena are apparently inscrutable; however, it is a notable fact that the strongest manifestations take place when the medium is in a

state of catalepsy, or suspended animation. Her hands are cold—her body becomes rigid—her eyes, if open, appear to be fixed on space—

A roll of thunder, quickly followed by a rush of wind, rudely interrupted my reading. The housekeeper appeared in the doorway, lamp in hand.

"Would you mind helping me close the windows, sir?" she asked. "There is a big rainstorm coming, and they must be closed quickly, or the furnishings and wall paper will be soaked."

Together we ascended the stairs. I rushed from window to window, while she lighted the way with the dim lamp. This duty attended to, she again bade me "Good night," and I returned to the living-room.

As I entered, I glanced at the casket: then looked again while a feeling of horror crept over me. Either I was dreaming, or it had been completely draped with a white sheet during my absence.

I rubbed my eyes, pinched myself, and advanced to confirm the evidence of my eyesight by the sense of touch. As I extended my hand, the center of the sheet rose in a sharp peak, as if lifted by some invisible presence, and the entire fabric traveled upward toward the ceiling. I drew back with a cry of dread, watching it with perhaps the same fascination that is experience by a doomed bird or animal looking the eyes of a serpent that is about to devour it.

The point touched the ceiling. There was a crash of thunder, accompanied by a blinding flash of lightning which illuminated the room through the sides of the ill-fitting window shades, and I found myself staring at the bare ceiling.

Walking dazedly to the fireplace, I poked the logs until they blazed, and then sat down to collect my thoughts. Torrents of rain were beating against the window panes. Thunder roared and lightning flashed incessantly.

I took up my pipe and was about to light it when a strange sight interrupted me. Something round and flat, about six inches in diameter, and of a grayish color, was moving along the floor from the casket toward the center of the room. I watched it, fascinated, while the blood seemed to congeal in my veins. It did not roll or slide along the floor, but seemed rather to *flow* forward.

It reminded me, more than anything else, of an amoeba, one of those microscopic, unicellular animalcule which I had examined in the study of zoology. An amoeba magnified perhaps, several million diameters. I could plainly see it put forth projections resembling pseudopods, form time to time, and again withdraw them quickly in the body mass.

The lighted match burned my fingers, and I dropped it on the hearth. In the meantime the creature had reached the center of the room and stopped. A metamorphosis was now taking place before my eyes. To my surprise, I beheld, in place of a magnified amoeba, a gigantic trilobite, larger, it is true, than any specimen which has ever been found, but, nevertheless, true to form in every detail.

The trilobite, in turn, changed to a brilliantly-hued starfish with active wriggling tentacles. The starfish became a crab, and the crab, a porpoise swimming about in the air as if it had been water. The porpoise then became a huge green lizard that crawled about the floor.

Soon the lizard grew large webbed wings, its tail shortened, its jaws lengthened out with a pelican-like pouch beneath them, and its body seemed partially covered with scales of a rusty black color. I afterward learned that this was a phantasmagorical representation of a pterodactyl, or prehistoric flying reptile. To me, in my terrified condition, it looked like a creature from hell.

The thing stood erect, stretched its wings and beat the air as if to try them; then rose and circled twice about the room, flapping lazily like a heron, and once more alighted in the middle of the floor.

It folded its wings carefully, and I noticed many new changes taking place. The scales were becoming feathers—the legs lengthened out and were encased in a thick, scaly, skin. The claws thickened into two-toed feet, like those of an ostrich. The head also looked ostrich-like, while the wings were shortened and feathered but not plumed. The bird was much larger than any ostrich or emu I have ever seen, and stalked about majestically, its head nearly touching the ceiling.

Soon it, too, stopped in the center of the room—the neck grew shorter and shorter—the feathers became fur—the wings lengthened into arms which reached below the knees, and I was face to face with a huge, gorilla-like creature. It roared horribly, casting quick glances about the room, its deepset eyes glowing like coals of fire.

I felt that my end had come, but could make no move to escape. I wanted to get up and leap through the window, but my nerveless limbs would not function. As I looked, the fur on the creature turned to a thin covering of hair, and it began to assume a manlike form. I closed my eyes and shuddered.

When I opened them a moment later, I beheld what might have been the "missing link," half man, half beast. The face, with its receding forehead and beetling brows, was apelike and yet manlike. Wrapped about its loins was a large tiger skin. In its right hand it brandished a huge, knitted club.

Gradually it became more manlike and less apelike. The club changed to a spear, the spear to a sword, and I beheld a Roman soldier, full accoutered for battle with helmet, armor, target and sandals.

The Roman soldier became a knight, and the knight a musketeer. The musketeer became a colonial soldier.

At that instant there was a crash of glass, and the branch of a tree projected through the windows on the right of the fireplace. The shade flew up with a snap and the soldier disappeared, as a brilliant flash of lightning illuminated the room.

I rushed to the window, and saw that the overhanging limb of an elm had been broken off by the wind and hurled through the glass. The rain was coming in in torrents.

The housekeeper, who had heard the noise, appeared in the doorway. Seeing the rain blowing in at the window, she left and returned a moment later with a hammer, tacks and a folded sheet. I tacked the sheet to the windows frame with difficulty, on account of the strong wind, and again pulled down the shade.

Mrs. Rhodes retired.

I consulted my watch. It lacked just one minute of midnight.

Only half of the night gone! Would I be strong enough to endure the other half?

CHAPTER 3

The storm slowly abated, and finally died down altogether, succeeded by a dead calm.

An hour passed without incident, to my inestimable relief. I believed that the phenomena had passed with the storm. The thought soothed me. I became drowsy, and was soon asleep.

Fitful dreams disturbed my slumber. It seemed that I was walking in a great primeval forest. The trees and vegetation about me were new and strange. Huge ferns, some of them fifty feet in height, grew all about in rank profusion. Under foot was a soft carpet of moss. Giant fungi, colossal toadstools, and mushrooms of varying shades and forms were everywhere.

In my hand I carried a huge knotted club, and my sole article of clothing seemed to be a tiger skin, girded about my waist and falling half way to my knees.

A queer-looking creature, half rhinoceros, half horse, ran across my pathway. Following closely behind it, in hot pursuit was a huge reptilian monster, in outline something like a kangaroo, in size larger than the largest elephant. Its monstrous serpent-like head towered more than twenty-five feet in the air as it suddenly stopped and stood erect on its hind feet and tail, apparently giving up the chase.

Then it spied me. Quick as a flash, I turned and ran, dodging hither and thither, floundering in the soft moss, stumbling over tangled vines and occasionally overturning a mammoth toadstool. I could hear the horrible beast crashing through the fern brakes, only a short distance behind me.

At last I came to a rocky hillside, and saw an opening about two feet in diameter. Into this I plunged headlong, barely in time to escape the frightful jaws which closed behind me with a terrifying *snap*. I lay on the ground, panting for breath, in the far corner of the cave and just out of reach of the ferocious monster. It appeared to be trying to widen the opening with its huge front feet...

Someone had laid a hand on my arm and was gently trying to awaken me. The cave and the horrible reptile disappeared, and I was again in my uncle's living-room. I turned, expecting to see Mrs. Rhodes, but saw no one.

There was, however, a hand on my arm. It ended at the wrist in a sort of indescribable, filmy mass. I was now fully awake, and somewhat startled, as may be imagined. The hand withdrew and seemed to float through the air to the other side of the room.

I now observed in the room a sort of white vapor, from which other hands were forming. Soon there were hands of all descriptions and sizes. They were constantly in motion, some of them flexing the fingers as if to try the newly-formed muscles, others beckoning, and still others clasped in pairs, as if in greeting.

There were large, horny masculine hands, daintily-formed womanly hands, and active, chubby little hands like those of children. Some of them were perfectly modeled. Others, apparently in the process of formation, looked like floating bits of chiffon, while still others had the appearance of flat, empty gloves.

Two well-developed hands now emerged from the mass and moved a few feet toward me. They waved as if attempting to attract my attention, and then I could see they were forming letters of the deaf and dumb alphabet. They spelled my name:

"B-I-L-L-Y."

Then:

"S-A-V-E M-E B-I-L-L-Y."

I managed to ask, "Who are you?"

The hands spelled:

"I A-M—"

Then they were withdrawn, with a jerk, into the group.

I could now see a new transformation taking place. The hands were drawn together, dissolving into a white, irregular fluted column, surmounted by a dark, hairy looking mass. A bearded face seemed to be forming at the top of the column, which was now widening out considerably, taking on the semblance of a human form. In a moment a white-robed figure stood there, the eyes turned upward and inward as if in fear and supplication, the arms extended toward me.

The apparition began slowly to advance in my direction. It seemed to glide along as if suspended in the air. There was no movement of walking, just a slow, floating motion.

The phantom, when at the other end of the room, had seemed frightful enough, but to see it coming toward me was unnerving— terrifying. The nearer it approached, the more horrible it seemed, and the more firmly I appeared rooted to the spot.

Soon it was towering above me. The eyes rolled downward and seemed to look through mine into my very brain. The arms were extended to encircle me, when the instinct of self-preservation came to my rescue.

I acted quickly, and apparently without volition. Overturning my chair and rushing from the room, I ran out the front door and down the pathway. I did not dare look back, but rushed blindly forth into the night.

Suddenly there was a brilliant glare of light. Something stuck me with considerable force, and I lost consciousness.

When I regained my senses I was lying in a bedroom, the room I had occupied in my uncle's house.

A beautiful girl was bending over me, bathing my fevered forehead from time to time with cold water. Sunlight was streaming in at the window. Outside, a robin was singing his morning song, his farewell to the Northland, no doubt, as the stinging snow-laden winds of winter must soon drive him southward.

I attempted to sit up, but sank back with a groan, as a sharp pain shot through my right side.

My fair attendant laid a soft hand on my brow.

"You mustn't do that again," she said. "The telephone wires are down, so father has driven to town for the doctor."

Memories of the night returned. The apparition—my rush down the pathway—the blinding light—the sudden shock—and then oblivion.

"Do you mind telling me," I asked, "what it was that knocked me out, and how you came so suddenly to my rescue?"

"It was our car that knocked you out," she replied, "and it was no more than right that I should do what I could to make you comfortable until the doctor arrives."

"Please tell me your name—won't you?—and how it all happened."

"My name is Ruth Randall. My father is Albert Randall, dean of the local college. We had motored to Indianapolis, intending to spend the weekend with friends, when we were notified of your uncle's death. He and my father were bosom friends, and together conducted many experiments in psychical research. Naturally we hurried home at once, in order to attend the funeral.

"We expected to make Peoria by midnight, but the storm came, and the roads soon were almost impassable. It was only by putting on chains and running at low speed most of the time that we were able to make any progress. Just as we were passing this house, you rushed in front of the car.

"Father says it is fortunate that we were compelled to run at low speed, otherwise you would have been instantly killed. We brought you to the door and aroused the housekeeper, who helped us get you to your room. Father tried to phone for a doctor, but it was no use, as the lines were torn down by the storm, so he drove to town for one. I think that is he coming now. I hear a motor in the driveway."

A few moments later two men entered—Professor Randall, tall, thin, slightly stooped, and pale of face, and Doctor Rush of medium height and rather portly. The doctor wore glasses with very thick lenses, through which he seemed almost to glare at me. He lost no time in taking my pulse and temperature, pushing the pocket thermometer into my mouth with one hand, and seizing my wrist with the other.

He removed the thermometer from my mouth, then, holding it up to the light and squinting for a moment said *"Humph,"* and proceeded to paw me over in search of broken bones. When he started manhandling my right side, I winced considerably. He presently located a couple of fractured ribs.

After a painful half-hour, during which the injured ribs were set, he left me with instructions to keep as still as possible, and let nature do the rest.

The professor lingered for a moment and I asked him to have Doctor Rush examine my uncle's body for signs of decomposition, as it was now more than three days since his death.

Miss Randall, who had left the room during the examination, came in just as her father was leaving, and said nice, sweet, sympathetic things, and fluffed up my pillow for me and smoothed back my hair; and if the doctor had taken my pulse at that moment he would have sworn my auricles and ventricles were racing each other for the world's championship.

"After all," I thought, "having one's ribs broken is not such an unpleasant experience."

Then her father, entered—and my thoughts were turned into new channels.

"Doctor Rush has made a thorough examination," he said, "and can find absolutely no sign of decomposition on your uncle's body. He frankly admits that he is puzzled by this condition, and that it is a case entirely outside his previous experience. He states that, from the condition of the corpse, he would have been led to believe that death took place only a few hours ago."

"If you can spare the time," I said, "and if it is not asking too much, I should like to have you spend the day with me. I have much to tell you, and many strange things have happened on which I sorely need your advice and assistance. Joe Severs can take the doctor home."

The professor kindly consented to stay, and his daughter went downstairs to locate Joe and his flivver.

"The things of which I am about to tell you," I began, "may seem like the visions of an opium eater, or the hallucinations of a deranged mind. In fact, they have even made me doubt by own sanity. However, I must tell someone, and as you are an old and valued friend of my uncle's, I feel that whether or not you accept my story as a verity you will be a sympathetic listener, and can offer some explanation—if, indeed, it be possible to explain such singular happenings."

I then related in detail everything that had happened since my arrival at the farm up to the moment when I rushed head long in front of his automobile.

He listened attentively, but whether he believed my narrative or not I could not tell. When I had finished, he asked many questions about the various phenomena I had witnessed, and seemed particularly interested when I told him about the disappearance of the bat. He asked me where the book, which had been used to dispatch the creature, might be found, and immediately went downstairs, bringing it up a moment later.

A dry, white smudge was still faintly discernible on the cover. This he examined carefully with a pocket microscope, then said:

"I will have to put this substance under a compound microscope, and also test it chemically in my laboratory. It may be the means of explaining all of the phenomena you have witnessed. I will drive home this afternoon and make a thorough examination of this sample."

"I should be very glad indeed," I replied, "to have even some slight explanation of these mysteries."

"You are undoubtedly aware," he said "that there are no vampires or similar bats indigenous to this part of the world. The only true vampire bat is found in South America, although there is a type of frugivorous bat slightly resembling it, which inhabits the southeast coast of Asia and Malayan Archipelago, and is sometimes erroneously called a vampire or specter bat. You have described in detail a creature greatly resembling the true vampire bat, but it is probable that what you saw was no bat at all. What it really was, I hesitate to say until I have examined the substance on this book cover."

"Well, whatever it was, I am positive it was no real vampire, as Glitch says," I replied.

"I don't like this vampire story that is being circulated by Glitch," said the professor. "It may lead to trouble. It is most surprising to find such crude superstition prevailing in these modern times."

At this juncture there was a rap at my door. I called, "come in," and Joe Severs entered.

"Well, Joe, did you get the doctor home without shaking any of his teeth loose?" I asked.

"Yes, sir, I got him home all right, but that ain't what I come to tell you about," he replied. "There's a heap of trouble brewin' around these parts an' I thought I better let you know. Somebody's sick in nearly every family in the neighborhood, an' they're sayin' Mr. Braddock is the cause of it. They're holdin' an indignation meetin' up to the school house now."

"This is indeed serious," said the professor. "Do you know what they propose to do about it?"

"Can't say as to that, but they're sure some riled up about it," replied Joe.

Mrs. Rhodes came in with my luncheon, and announced to the professor that Miss Ruth awaited him in the dining-room below, whereupon he begged to be excused. Joe went out murmuring something about having to feed the horses, and I was left alone to enjoy a very tasty meal.

CHAPTER 4

A half hour later the housekeeper came in to remove the dishes, and Miss Randall brought me a huge bouquet of autumn daisies.

"Father has driven to town to analyze a sample of something or other that he has found," she said, "and in the meantime I will do my best to make the hours pass pleasantly for you. What do you want me to do? Shall I read to you?"

"By all means," I replied. "Read or talk, or do anything you like. I assure you I am not hard to amuse."

"I think I shall read," she decided. "What do you prefer? fiction, history, mythology, philosophy? Or perhaps," she added, "you prefer poetry."

"I will leave the selection entirely to you," I said. "Read what interests you, and I will be interested."

"Don't be too sure of that," she answered, and went down to my uncle's library.

She returned a few moments later with several volumes. From a book of Scott's poems, she chose "Rokeby" and soon we were conveyed, as if by a magic carpet, to medieval Yorkshire with its moated castles, dense forests, sparkling streams, jutting crags and enchanted dells.

She had finished the poem, and we were chatting gaily, when Mrs. Rhodes entered.

"A small boy brought this note for you, sir," she said, handing me a sealed envelope.

I tore it open carelessly, then read:

Mr. William Ansley.

Dear Sir:

"Owing to the fact that at least one member of nearly every family in this community has been smitten with peculiar malady, in some instances fatal, since the death of James Braddock, and in view of the undeniable evidence that the corpse of the aforesaid had become a vampire, proven by certain things which you, in company with two respected and veracious neighbors witnessed, an indignation meeting was held today, attended by more than one hundred residents, for the purpose of discussing ways and means of combating this terrible menace to the community.

"Tradition tells us that there are two effective ways for disposing of a vampire. One is by burning the corpse of the offender, the other is by burial with a stake driven through the heart. We have decided on the latter as the more simple and easily carried out.

"You are therefore directed to convey the corpse to the pine grove which is situated a half mile back from the road on your uncle's farm, where you will find a grave ready dug, and six men who will see that the body is properly interred. You have until eight o'clock his evening to carry out these instructions.

"To refuse to do as directed will avail you nothing. If you do not bring the body we will come and get it. If you offer resistance, you do so at your peril, as we are armed, and we mean business.
                                                    THE COMMITTEE.

P.S. No use to try to telephone or send a messenger for help. Your wires are out of commission and the house is surrounded by armed sentinels.

As the professor had predicted, this was indeed a most serious turn of events. I turned to Mrs. Rhodes.

"Where is the bearer of this letter?' I asked. "Did he wait for a reply?"

"It was given to me by a small boy." she answered. "He said that if you wished to reply, to put your letter in the mailbox, and it would be given to the right party. There was a closed automobile waiting for him in front of the house, and he ran back to it and was driven away at high speed."

"I must dress and go downstairs at once," I said.

"You must do no such thing," replied Miss. Randall. "The doctor's orders are that you must keep perfectly quiet until your ribs heal."

I heard a swift footfall on the stairs, and a moment later the professor entered the room, very much excited.

"Two farmers," he said, "poked shotguns in my face and searched me on the public highway. That's what just happened to me!"

"What do you suppose they were after?" I asked.

"They did not make themselves clear on that point, and they didn't take anything, so I am at a loss to explain their conduct. They merely stopped me, felt through my pockets and searched the car: then told me to drive on."

"Perhaps this will throw some light on their motive," I said, handing him the letter.

As he read it a look of surprise came over his face.

"Ah! It is quite plain, now. These were the armed guards mentioned in the postscript. It seems incredible that such superstition should prevail in this enlightened age; however, the evidence is quite too plain to be questioned. What is to be done?"

"Frankly, I don't know," I replied. "We are evidently so well watched that it would be impossible for anyone to go for help. Of course, they cannot harm my deceased uncle by driving a stake through the corpse, but to permit these barbarians to carry out their purpose would be to desecrate the memory of the best friend I ever had."

"What are they going to do?" asked Miss Randall in alarm. I handed her the letter. She read it hastily, then ran downstairs to see if the telephone was working.

"What would you say if I were to tell you there is a strong possibility that your uncle's body is *not* a corpse; or, in other words, that he is not *really dead?*" asked the professor.

"I would say that if there is the slightest possibility of that, they will make a corpse of me before they stage this vampire funeral," I replied, starting to dress.

"I am with you in that," said he, extending his hand, "and now let us examine the evidence."

"By all means," I answered.

"According to the belief of most modern psychologists," he began, "every human being is endowed with two minds. Ones is usually termed the objective, or conscious mind, the other the subjective, or subconscious mind. Some call it the subliminal consciousness. The former controls our waking hours, the latter is dominant when we are asleep.

"You are, no doubt, familiar with the functions and powers of the objective mind, so we will not discuss them. The powers of the subjective mind, which are not generally known or recognized, are what chiefly concern us in this instance.

"My belief that your uncle is not really dead started when I first heard your story. It was later substantiated by two significant facts. I will take up the various points in their logical order, and you may judge for yourself as to whether or not my hypothesis is fully justified.

"First, upon seeing him lying in the casket, you involuntarily exclaimed, 'He is not dead—only sleeping.' This apparently absurd statement, unsubstantiated by objective evidence, was undoubtedly prompted by your subjective mind. One of the best know powers of the subjective mind is that of telepathy, the communication of thoughts or ideas form mind to mind, without the employment of physical means. This message was apparently impressed so strongly on your subjective mind that you spoke it aloud, automatically, almost without the subjective knowledge that you were talking. Assuming that it was a telepathic message, it must necessarily have been projected by *some other mind.* May we not, therefore, reasonably supposed that the message came from the subjective mind of you uncle?

"Then the second message. Was it not plainly from someone who knew you intimately, someone in dire need? You will recall that, just before you fell asleep, you seemed to hear the words, '*Billy! Save me, Billy.*'

"And now, as to the phenomena: I must confess that I was somewhat in doubt, at first, regarding these. Not that I questioned your veracity in the least, for no man rushed blindly in front of a moving automobile without sufficient cause, but the sights which you witnessed were so striking and unusual that I felt sure they must have been hallucinations. On second thought, however, I decided that it would be quite out of the ordinary for you and two other men to have the same hallucinations. It was therefore, apparent that you had witnessed genuine materialization phenomena.

"The key to the whole situation, however, lay in the seemingly insignificant smudge on the book cover. Two years ago your uncle advanced a theory that materialization phenomena were produced by a substance which he termed 'psychoplasm.' After listening to his argument, I was convinced that he was right. Since then, we have attended numerous materialization seances, with the object of securing a sample of this elusive material for examination. It always disappears instantly when bright light is flashed upon it, or when the medium is startled or alarmed, and our efforts in this direction have always been fruitless.

"Needless to say, when you described the deposit left on the book by the phantasmagorical bat, I was intensely interested. Microscopic examination and analysis show that this substance is something quite different from anything I have ever encountered. While it is undoubtedly organic, it is nevertheless remarkably different, in structure and composition, from anything heretofore classified, either by biologists or chemists. In short, I am convinced it is that substance which has eluded us for so long, namely, psychoplasm.

"No doubt you will wonder what bearing this has on the question under discussion—that is, whether or not your uncle still lives. As far as we are able to learn, psychoplasm is produced only by, or through, *living* persons, and in nearly every instance it occurs only when the person acting as medium is in a state of catalepsy, or suspended animation. As most of the manifestations took place in the room where your uncle's body lay, and as he is the only one in the house likely to be in that state, I assume that your uncle's soul still inhabits his body.

"The final point, and by no means the least important is that in spite of the time which has elapsed since his alleged death—in spite of that fact that it lay in a warm room without refrigeration or embalming fluid—our uncle's body shows absolutely no sign of decomposition."

"But how is it possible," I asked, "for a person in a cataleptic stated to simulate death so completely as to deceive the most competent physicians?"

"How such a thing is possible, I cannot explain any more than I can tell you how psychoplasm is generated. The wonderful powers of the subjective entity are truly amazing. We can only deal with the facts as we find them. Statistics show that no less that one case a week of suspended animation is discovered in the United States. There are, no doubt, hundreds of other cases which are never brought to light. As a usual thing, nowadays, the doctor no sooner pronounces the patient dead than the undertaker is summoned. Needless to say, when the arteries have been drained and the embalming fluid injected, there is absolutely no chance of the patient coming to life."

Together, we walked downstairs and entered the room where Uncle Jim lay. We looked carefully, minutely, for some sign of life, but none was apparent.

"It is useless," said the professor, "to employ physical means at this time. However, I have an experiment to propose, which, if successful, may prove my theory. As I stated previously, you are, no doubt, subjectively in mental *en rapport* with your uncle. Your subjective mind constantly communicates with his, but you lack the power to elevate the messages to your objective consciousness. My daughter has cultivated to some extent the power of automatic writing. You can, no doubt, establish rapport with her by touch. I will put the questions."

Miss Randall was called, and upon our explaining to her that we wished to conduct an experiment in automatic writing, she readily consented. Her father seated her at the library table, with pencil and paper near her right hand. He then held a small hand mirror before her, slight above the level of her eyes, on which she fixed her gaze.

When she had looked steadily at the mirror for a short time he made a few hypnotic passes with his hands, whereupon she closed her eyes and apparently fell into a light sleep. Then, placing the pencil in her right hand, he told me to be seated beside her, and place my right hand over her left. We sat thus for perhaps ten minutes, when she began to write, very slowly at first, then gradually increasing in speed until the pencil fairly flew over the paper. When the bottom of the sheet had been reached a new one was supplied, and this was half covered with writing before she stopped.

The professor and I examined the resulting manuscript. Something about it seemed strangely familiar to me. I remember seeing those words in a book I had picked up in that same room. On making a comparison, we found that she had written, word for word, the introduction to my uncle's book, "The Reality of Materialization Phenomena."

"We will now ask some questions," said the professor.

He took a pencil and paper and made a record of his questions the answers to which were written by his daughter. I have copied them verbatim, and present them below.

Q: "Who are you that writes?"
A: "Ruth."
Q: "By whose direction do you write?"
A: "Billy."
Q: "Who directs Billy to direct you to write as you do?"
A: "Uncle Jim."
Q: "How are we to know that it is Uncle Jim?"
A: "Uncle Jim will give proof."
Q: "If Uncle Jim will tell us something which he knows and we do not know, but which we can find out, he will have furnished sufficient proof. What can Uncle Jim tell us?"

A: "Remove third book from left top shelf of book case. Shake book and pressed maple leaf will fall out."

(The professor removed and shook it as directed, and a pressed maple leaf fell to the floor.)

Q: "What further proof can Uncle Jim give?"

A: "Get key from small urn on mantle. Open desk in corner and take out small ledger. Turn to page sixty and find account of Peoria Grain Company. Account balanced October first by check for one thousand two hundred forty-eight dollars and sixty-three cents."

(Again the professor did as directed, and again the written statement was corroborated.)

Q: "The proof is ample and convincing. Will Uncle Jim tell us where he is at the present time?"

A: "Here in the room."

Q: "What means shall we use to awaken him?"

A: "Uncle Jim is recuperating. Does not wish to be awakened."

Q: "But we want Uncle Jim to waken some time. What shall we do?"

A: "Let Uncle Jim alone, and he will waken naturally when the time comes."

The professor propounded several more queries, to which there were no answers, so we discontinued the sitting. Miss Randall was awakened by suggestion.

"We now have conclusive proof that your uncle is alive, and in a cataleptic state," said the professor.

"Is there no way to arouse him?" I asked.

"The best thing to do is to let him waken himself, as he directed us to do in the telepathic message. He is, as he says, recuperating from his illness and should not be disturbed. You are, perhaps, unaware that catalepsy, although believed by many people to be a disease, is really no disease at all. While it is known as a symptom of certain nervous disorders, it may accompany any form of sickness, or may even be caused by a mental or physical shock of some sort.

"It can also be induced in hypnotization by suggestion. Do not think of it as a form of sickness, but, rather, as a very deep sleep, which permits the patient much needed rest for an overburdened body and mind; for it is a well-known fact that when catalepsy intervenes in any form of sickness, death is usually cheated."

"Would it be dangerous to my uncle's health if we were to remove him to his bedroom?" I asked. "It seems to me that a coffin is rather a gruesome thing for him to convalesce in"

"Agreed," said the professor, "and I can see no particular harm in moving him, provided he is handled very gently. Ruth, will you please have Mrs. Rhodes make the room ready? Mr. Ansley and I will then carry his uncle upstairs."

While Miss Randall was doing her father's bidding we tried to contrive a way to outwit the superstitious farmers, who would arrive in a few minutes if they made good their threat.

My eye fell upon two large oak logs, which young Severs had brought for the fireplace, and I said,

"Why not weight the casket with these logs and screw the lid down? No doubt they will carry it out without opening it, and when they are well on their way we can place my uncle in your car and be out of reach before they discover the substitution."

"A capital idea," said the professor. "We will wrap the logs well so they will not rattle, and, as the casket is an especially heavy one, they will be non the wiser until it is opened at the grave."

I ran upstairs and tore two heavy comforters from my bed, and with these we soon had the logs well padded. Miss Randall called that the room was ready. The professor and I carefully lifted my uncle from the casket and were about to take him from the room, when a gruff voice commanded:

"Schtop!"

A dozen masked men, armed indiscriminately with shotguns, rifles and revolvers, were standing in the hall. We could hear the stamping of many more on the porch. I recognized the voice and figure of the leader of those of Glitch.

"Back in der coffin," he said, pointing a double-barreled shotgun at me. "Poot him back, or I blow your tam head off."

Then several other men came in and menaced us with their weapons.

CHAPTER 5

I dropped my uncle's feet and rushed furiously at Glitch, but was quickly seized and overpowered by two stalwart farmers.

The professor, however, was more calm. He laid my uncle gently on the floor and faced the men.

"Gentlemen," he said, "may I ask the reason for this sudden and unwarranted intrusion in a peaceful home?"

"Ve are going to bury dot vampire corpse wit a stake t'rough its heart. Dot's vot," replied Glitch.

"What would you do if I were to tell you that this man is not dead, but alive?" asked the professor.

"Alive or dead, he's gonna be buried tonight," said a burly ruffian, stepping up to my uncle. "One o' you guys help me get this in the coffin."

A tall, lean farmer stepped up and leaned his gun against the casket. The the two of them roughly lifted my uncle into it and screwed down the lid.

In the meantime, another had discovered the wrapped logs, to which he call the attention of his companions.

"Well, I'll be blowed!" he said. "Thought yuh was pretty slick, didn't yuh? Thought yuh could fool us with a coupla logs? Just for that we'll take yuh along to the part so yuh don't try no more fancy capers."

"Gentlemen," said the professor, "do you realize that you will be committing a murder if you bury this man's body?"

"Murder, Hell!" exclaimed one. "He killed my boy."

"He sucked my daughter's blood," cried another.

"An' my brother is lyin' in his death bed on account of him," shouted a third.

"Come one, let's go," said the burly ruffian. "Some o' you boys grab hold o' them handles, an' we'll change shifts goin' out."

"Yah. Ve vill proceed," said Glitch. "Vorwarts!"

"If you will permit me, I will go and reassure my daughter before accompanying you," said the professor. "She is very nervous and may be prostrated with fear if I do not calm her."

"Go ahead and be quick about it," said the ruffian. "Don't try no funny stunts, though, or we'll use the stake on you, too"

The professor hurried upstairs and, on his return a moment later, the funeral cortege proceeded.

It was pitch dark outside, and therefore necessary for some of the men to carry lanterns. One of these led the way. Immediately after him walked six men bearing the casket, behind which the professor and I walked with an armed guard on either side of us.

Following, we were the remainder of the men, some twenty-five all told. There was no talking, except at intervals when the pallbearers were relieved by others. This occurred a number of times, as the burden was heavy and the way none too smooth.

I walked as one in a trance. It seemed that my feet moved automatically, as if directed by a power outside myself. Sometimes I thought it all a horrible nightmare from which I should presently awaken. Then the realization of the terrible truth would come to me, engendering a grief that seemed unbearable.

I mentally reviewed the many kindnesses of my uncle. I thought of his generous self-sacrifice, that I might be educated to cope with the world; and now that the time had come when I should be of service to him—when his very life was to be taken—I was failing him, failing miserably.

I cudgeled my numb brain for some way of outwitting the superstitious farmers. Once I thought of wrestling the gun from my guard and fighting the mob alone, but I knew this would be useless. I would merely delay, not defeat, the grisly plans of these men, and would be almost sure to lose my own life in the attempt. I was faint and weak, and my broken ribs pained incessantly.

All too soon, we arrived at the pine grove, and moved toward a point from which the rays of a lantern glimmered faintly through the trees. A few moments more, and we were beside a shallow grave at which the six grim sextons, masked like their companions, waited.

The casket was placed in the grave and the lid removed. Then a long, stout stake, sharply pointed with iron, was brought forward, and two men with heavy sledges moved, one to each side of the grave.

Here a discussion arose as to whether it would be better to drive the stake through the body and then replace the lid, or to put the lid on first and then drive the stake through the entire coffin. The latter plan was finally decided upon, and the lid replaced, when we were all startled by a terrible screaming coming from a thicket, perhaps a hundred yards distant. It was the voice of a woman in mortal terror.

"*Help!* Save me—save me!" she cried. "Oh, my God, will nobody save me?"

In a moment, all was confusion. Stake and mauls were dropped, and everyone rushed toward the thicket. The cries redoubled as we approached. Presently we saw a woman running through the underbrush, and after a chase of several minutes over took her. My heart leaped to my throat as I recognized Ruth Randall.

She was crouching low, as if in deadly fear of something which she seemed to be trying to push away from her—something invisible, imperceptible, to us. Her beautiful hair hung below her waist, and her clothing was bedraggled and torn.

I was first to reach her side.

"Ruth! What is the matter?"

"Oh, that huge bat—that terrible bat with the fiery eyes! Drive him away from me! Don't let him get me! Please! *Please!*"

I tried to soothe her in my arms. She looked up, her eyes distended with terror.

"There he is—right behind you! Oh, don't let him get me! Please don't let him get me!"

I looked back, but could see nothing resembling a bat. The armed men stood around us in a circle.

"There is no bat behind me." I said. "You are overwrought. Don't be frightened."

"But there *is* a bat. I can *see* him. He is flying around us in a circle now. Don't you see him flying there?" and she described an arc with her hand. "You men have guns. Shoot him. Drive him away."

Glitch spoke, "It's der vampire again. Ve'll put a schtop to dis business right now. Come one, men."

We started back to the grove. I was nonplussed—mystified. Perhaps there was such a thing as a vampire, after all. But no, that could not be. She was only the victim of overwrought nerves.

Once more we stood beside the grave. Two men were screwing down the coffin lid. The three with the stake and sledges stood ready. I saw that Miss Randall was trembling with the cold, for she had come out without a wrap, and, removing, my coat, I placed it around her.

The professor stood at the foot of the grave, looking down calmly at the men. He appeared almost unconcerned.

The stake was placed on the spot, calculated to be directly above the left breast of my uncle, and the man nearest me raised his sledge to strike.

I leaped toward him.

"Don't strike! For God's sake, don't strike!" I cried, seizing his arm.

Someone hit me on the back of the head, and strong arms dragged me back. My senses reeled, as I saw first one heavy sledge descend, then another. The stake crashed through the coffin and deep into the ground beneath, driven by the relentless blows.

Suddenly, apparently from the bottom of the grave, came a muffled wailing cry, increasing to a horrible, blood-curdling shriek.

The mob stood for a moment as if paralyzed, then, to a man, fled precipitately, stopping for neither weapons nor tools. I found temporary relief in unconsciousness....

My senses returned to me gradually. I was walking, or, rather, reeling, as one intoxicated, between Miss Randall and her father, who were helping me toward the house. The professor was carrying a lantern which one of the men had dropped and fantastic, swaying, bobbing shadows stretched wherever its rays penetrated.

After what seemed an age of painful travel we reached the house, Miss Randall helped me into the front room, the professor following. Sam and Joe Severs were there, and someone reclined in the large morris chair facing the fire. Mrs. Rhodes came bustling in with a steaming tea wagon.

I moved toward the fire, for I was chilled through. As I did so, I glanced toward the occupant of the morris chair, then gave a startled cry.

The man in the chair was Uncle Jim!

"Hello, Billy," he said. "How are you, my boy?"

For a moment I was speechless. "Uncle Jim!" I managed to stammer. "Is it really you, or am I dreaming again?"

Ruth squeezed my arm reassuringly. "Don't be afraid. It is really your uncle."

I knelt by the chair and felt Uncle Jim's arm about my shoulders. "Yes, it is really I, Billy. A bit weak and shaken, perhaps, but I'll soon be as sound as a new dollar."

"But how—when—how did you get out of that horrible grave?"

"First I will ask Miss Ruth if she will be so kind as to preside over the tea wagon. Then I believe my friend Randall can recount the events of the evening much more clearly and satisfactorily than I."

"Being, perhaps, more familiar with the evening's deep-laid plot than some of those present, I accept the nomination," replied the professor, smiling, "although, in doing so, I do not want to detract one iota from the honor due to my fellow plotters for their most efficient assistance, without which my plan would have been a complete failure."

Tea was served, cigars were lighted, and the professor began.

"In the first place, I am sure you will all be interested in knowing the cause of the epidemic on account of which some of our neighbors have reverted to the superstition of the dark ages. It is explained by an article in *The Peoria Times*, which I brought with me this afternoon, but did not have time to read until a moment ago, which states that the countryside is being swept by a new and strange malady known as 'sleeping sickness,' and that physicians have not, as yet, found any efficient means of combating the disease.

"Now for this evening's little drama. You will, no doubt, recall, Mr Ansley, that before we joined the funeral procession, I requested a moment's conversation with my daughter. The events which followed were the result of that conversation.

"In order that the plan might be carried out, it was necessary for her first to gain the help of Joe and Sam here, and then make a quick detour around the procession. I know that there are few men who will not rush to the rescue of a woman in distress and I asked her to call for help in order to divert the mob from the grave. She thought of the bat idea herself, and I must say it worked most excellently.

"While everyone was gone, Joe and Sam, who had stationed themselves nearby, came and helped me remove your uncle from the casket. As we did so, I noticed signs of returning consciousness, brought about in some measure, no doubt, by the rude jolting of the casket. Then the boys carried him to the house, while I replaced the lid. You are all familiar with what followed."

"But that unearthly shriek from the grave," I said. "It sounded like the cry of a dying man."

"Ventriloquism," said the professor, "nothing more. A simple little trick I learned in my high school days. It was I who shrieked."

* * * *

Uncle Jim and I convalesced together.

When my ribs were knitted and his strength was restored, it was decided that he should go to Florida for the winter, and that I should have charge of the farm. He said that my education and training should make me a far more capable manager than he, and that the position should be mine as long as I desired it.

He delayed his trip, however, until a certain girl, who had made me a certain promise, exchanged the name of Randall for that of Ansley. Then he left us to our happiness.

www.ingramcontent.com/pod-product-compliance
Lightning Source LLC
Chambersburg PA
CBHW030635130626
46552CB00002B/865